The Messengers

GEORGES-OLIVIER

CHÂTEAUREYNAUD

The Messengers

TRANSLATED BY

EDWARD GAUVIN

WAKEFIELD PRESS

CAMBRIDGE, MASSACHUSETTS

Wakefield Press, P.O. Box 425645, Cambridge, MA 02142

Originally published as *Les Messagers* in 1974, then revised and republished in 1990.

This book was set in Garamond Premier Pro and Helvetica Neue Pro by Wakefield Press. Printed and bound by Versa Press in the United States of America.

ISBN: 978-1-939663-99-3

Available through D.A.P./Distributed Art Publishers
75 Broad Street, Suite 630
New York, New York 10004
Tel: (212) 627-1999
Fax: (212) 627-9484

10 9 8 7 6 5 4 3 2 1

TRANSLATOR'S INTRODUCTION

> The messenger immediately sets out on his journey; a powerful, an indefatigable man; now pushing with his right arm, now with his left, he cleaves a way for himself through the throng; if he encounters resistance he points to his breast, where the symbol of the sun glitters; the way is made easier for him than it would be for any other man. But the multitudes are so vast; their numbers have no end.
>
> Franz Kafka, "An Imperial Message,"
> trans. Willa and Edwin Muir

Kafka is one of only two authors to whom Marcel Schneider, in his *Histoire de la littérature fantastique en France*, devotes an entire chapter. (The other is Edgar Allan Poe; both are foreign, perhaps tacitly corroborating the complaint, oft bandied about, that the Cartesian duality of the default French mindset does not readily admit of the fantastic.) Almost forty years after its definitive version, Schneider's tome remains an authoritative overview of

Francophone contributions to the genre. A scholar and fantasist himself, he charts a clear if crooked lineage from E. T. A. Hoffmann to Poe to Kafka, each an evolution in the French notion of the fantastic that marked an immune reaction of native rationalism to a powerful and pervasive foreign intervention. Kafka he calls a *bombe à retardement*. Perhaps we may seek farther than the first translation at hand, "time bomb," for one that places, like the French, less emphasis on countdown and more on excruciating, seditious deferment, a translation fortuitously specific to the period in question and since fallen from use: "delay-action bomb." Though translations of the Czech insurance agent began dropping in the 1930s—Alexandre Vialatte in France, Anita Rho in Italy, the Muirs in England and America—Schneider dates the start of Kafka's "ravages" to the immediate aftermath of the Second World War. To hear Schneider tell it, one might think it took the Nazis to make bureaucracy more convincing. "Let us admire," he writes, "the fact that so allegorical, symbolic, and secretive a body of work could have become the mirror of our own world: inconceivable before the 1940s, and seemingly self-evident ever since."[1] The first recorded use of "Kafkaesque" dates to this same postwar period. The scope of Kafka's influence soon becomes apparent in works by Walter Jens, Dino Buzzati, and Maurice Blanchot, to the extent that in 1946, *Action*, the weekly of the French intelligentsia, asks: "Must Kafka be burned?" Too soon, *Action*, too soon . . . The next year, Georges-Olivier Châteaureynaud was born in a liberated Paris where, at a Victory Ball, his young mother had met his father, freshly returned from Sachsenhausen-Oranienburg, emaciated and short a few teeth.

With *A Life on Paper*, the volume of selected stories from Small Beer Press that introduced him to American readers in 2010,

Georges-Olivier Châteaureynaud was hailed by the *Believer* as a "master craftsman" and by *Three Percent*, *Time Out*, and the *Times Literary Supplement* as a successor to Poe, Nikolai Gogol, and Kafka. Fabulist John Crowley, winner of an American Academy of Arts and Letters Award for Literature, placed him in "the secret brotherhood that has only exemplars, no definition: Kafka, Bruno Schulz, Nathanael West, Aimee Bender."[2] The ever-inventive Brian Evenson hailed him as a "focused writer pursuing a personal and highly individual oneiric project,"[3] and in the *New York Times*, Jeff VanderMeer praised his "graceful, penetrating stories" that "linger on the edge of darkness and absurdity."[4] In proclaiming that "beautiful prose featuring ingenuous protagonists and clever, unexpected forays into horror are the hallmarks of these mischievous stories,"[5] *Publishers Weekly* neatly summed up the general acclaim for the long-overdue debut of a figure central not only to reviving the short story in France but also to sustaining a tradition for which France is little known abroad: the fantastic.

The Messengers was Châteaureynaud's first novel, published the year after his 1973 debut collection *Le Fou dans la chaloupe* (The madman in the dinghy). Awarded a short-lived prize from *Nouvelles Littéraires*, it secured the author publicity, a special issue of the eponymous magazine, and the then-princely sum of 50,000 francs, which enabled his purchase of a used Renault that, though its doors had to be bungeed together from within to keep from flapping open, nonetheless proved of great aid in his day job (one of several) as a rag-and-bone man. It has become, among Châteaureynaud's works, something of a cult favorite kept continuously in print by small presses—La Table Ronde, Actes Sud's Babel imprint—though the pared-down 1990 version differs significantly from the prizewinning original. As John Taylor notes in his first volume of *Paths to Contemporary French Literature*, "The more than 1,500 deletions and minor stylistic changes made by the author in this disquieting text have transformed a remarkable first novel into a masterly novella."[6] It is this novella that, more than three decades later, here makes its way into English.

Its events are simple, symbolic. For as long as he can remember, the messenger has carried a message in the satchel on his back. He has never read it, nor does he know whom it is meant for; every seeming recipient proves to be not an end to his journey but a further relay in a chain referring him ever and exhaustingly onward. There is something of the automaton, not to say the demonic, about this driven man, into whose orbit comes a hapless, aimless, vagabond youth, most recently on the run for careless crimes. Nothing matters to the man but his mission; to fulfill it he will without hesitation forsake, murder, and betray. The youth simply has nothing to better to do—with his time, his life—and starved for even a scrap of human affection, he falls in with this least fitting of mentors, his blunted understanding mercilessly conscripted by the messenger's unyielding commitment to obscure purpose. This Beckettian setup plays out in a picaresque structure as the pair travel from rural manor to urban mansion, from endless vaulted cellars of suspended iron cages to a brothel of unsettling ritual on an island in the middle of a wooded lake—settings dimly reminiscent of traditional adventure, here warped and transfigured by a pervading atmosphere of ever-incipient and rarely full-fledged nightmare.

It is no secret that *The Messengers* is Châteaureynaud's most nakedly Kafkaesque work. Schneider notes as much, as does the *Histoire de la littérature française de 1940 à nos jours* by Jacques

Brenner—writer, critic, and incidentally, the editor at Grasset who acquired *Le Fou dans la chaloupe*. Châteaureynaud himself groups *The Messengers* unequivocally with "une littérature noire."[7] In an interview with Jean-Luc Moreau, the author asserts, "The core of my characters' thinking and of my own is that the human condition is horror, pure and simple. What's more, I tend to believe you stay an artist so long as you keep that in mind, bear subterranean witness to it."[8] *The Messengers* is more violent and less forgiving than his later work, told in a voice deliberately flatter than the voluble and ironic one that has come to dominate his short stories. A chill pervades this book, awash in grays. Its characters are constantly in uncomprehending motion—restless, even frenetic in their unfulfillment. The destruction they perpetrate is both callous and collateral. Fate, or fatedness, lies heavy as an edict over them, yet what fate, exactly? In lieu of reply, Châteaureynaud gives us bewilderment distilled to its essence of fearful alienation, yet also elevated to existential tenet. This book—in its mineral hermeticism, its curatorial descriptions, its abrupt monologues at once plaintive and plangent, its air of stifling opacity maintained by a flat refusal to psychologize—offers a rather pitiless vision of human endeavor: mystery, duty, momentum, undoing. Inevitably, the message outlives the man; the messenger is dead, long live the messenger.

Speaking of messages, there's something of a love affair between French and English literature, especially where the fantastic is concerned. French Decadents were reflected in the dark mirror of their British brethren and in the American "weird tale," a somber hybrid of fantasy and horror. But why should the last communiqués from French shores date more than a century back, or to the Surrealists at best? These traditions, twinned at birth and lost more in transit than translation, have as much to learn from their independent evolutions as from their history of mutual influence.

Often grouped with Jorge Luis Borges, Alfred Kubin, and Gustav Meyrink, Châteaureynaud also brings his own university studies in British literature to his work, often citing Robert Louis Stevenson, Mary Shelley, and H. G. Wells. His oeuvre inhabits the interstices of multiple traditions and movements, from the medieval marvelous to Jules Verne's "vulgarisations" and Marcel Aymé's Gallic whimsy, bringing to light intertwinings of literary histories forgotten or overlooked in the current French landscape. His classically inflected *fantastique* descends directly from the *conte*, the European oral tradition of folk and fairy tale, through the Decadents and their *contes cruels*, cited as influences by such contemporary genre-bending movements of literary fantasy as the New Weird. His sense of the marvelous is fully inflected by the legacy of Surrealism—scholarship on which, as historian Gavin Parkinson observes, has focused almost exclusively on the 1920s and 1930s instead of the post–World War II period. However, Surrealism continued to inform the French fantastic even as the latter drew new life from continental fabulism (Italo Calvino, Buzzati, Tommaso Landolfi), which married folklore with experimental form; the South American magic realism of cosmopolitan expatriates (Octavio Paz, Borges, Julio Cortázar); and the manic inventions of a largely Anglophone import, the genre marketed as science fiction and fantasy.

In 1992, critic Jean-Luc Moreau published a "manifesto-cum-anthology" titled after the brief movement he was about to found: *La Nouvelle Fiction*. It was, wrote Taylor, "the most ambitious theoretical attempt since Alain Robbe-Grillet's *Pour un nouveau roman*

(1963) to define the affinities and literary aspirations of a group of French writers [and] an appellation . . . accepted, by the writers, with a unanimity never attained in the cases of, say, Surrealism or the New Novel."[9] All prestigious prizewinners publishing for over two decades, the seven authors assembled—among them Châteaureynaud—shared "a literary heritage of German romanticism, the English gothic novel, the oriental tale, spiritualism, speculative philosophy, and Surrealism . . . represent[ing] an aesthetic that differs considerably from those practiced by other prominent groups in French writing." In its insistence on the expansive and gloriously counterfactual character of narrative, La Nouvelle Fiction offers points of intersection with our own riotous metafictioneers (Robert Coover, John Barth, Donald Barthelme).

Unmistakably literary in his style and milieu (Renaudot, Goncourt, Académie Française prizes), Châteaureynaud unites the highbrow and popular, winning the 2008 Grand Prix de l'Imaginaire at the international festival of speculative fiction, Utopiales, for his novel *L'Autre rive*—the first volume in a trilogy French critics called "Balzac directed by Jean-Pierre Jeunet or Tim Burton." Over the course of eleven novels, ten story collections, and countless chapbooks, he has broadened and deepened the literary possibilities of the fantastic, a key figure in charting the latter-day developments of its largely ignored French evolutions. So often an inveterate and unapologetic nostalgist, Châteaureynaud in *The Messengers* nevertheless braids a longing for the lost worlds of Alain-Fournier with Stevensonian adventure and something altogether more enigmatic and impenetrable. "The aim of literature that interests me," claims Châteaureynaud, "is the abyss."[10]

Over the past decade, Wakefield Press, taking up the mantle from such stalwarts as Atlas Press and Exact Change, has steadily, surreptitiously curated a catalog of "overlooked gems and literary oddities," the obscure and forgotten, yes, but also the eccentric, orphaned, and unbeloved—grotesqueries, railleries, and hauntings; ironies, idleries, and irrealities. What better home for the French fantastic? By reinventing literatures, we reinvent nations. By making new work available, we create new readerships, and teach readers, old and new alike, to read differently. This body of work deserves to be brought to light: a lost continent with global appeal. Just as fantasy itself can speculate in alternate histories, so Francophone fabulism presents an underside to standard twentieth-century literary histories, eschewing the usual literary and critical landmarks. A milestone in the field, *The Messengers* is an overdue letter between two long-divided lovers once close, but fallen largely out of touch, a *billet doux* to rekindle the relationship between the French and English fantastic. And yet . . . how futile are our efforts. "If he succeeded in that, nothing would be gained . . ." Kafka's caveat to his messenger's conjectured progress echoes through the architectures concatenated in his parable's concluding clauses: chambers, palaces, courts, gates, capitals, sediment. Who is to say our missives do not leave our hands only for the abyss? Still, we sit at our windows as evening falls, and dream. All translation is a *bombe à retardement*.

NOTES

1. Marcel Schneider, *Histoire de la littérature fantastique en France* (Paris: Fayard, 1985), 418. My translation.

2. Blurb from Georges-Olivier Châteaureynaud, *A Life on Paper: Stories*, tr. Edward Gauvin (Easthampton: Small Beer Press, 2010).

3. Châteaureynaud, *A Life on Paper*, ii.

4. Jeff VanderMeer, "Science Fiction Chronicle," *The New York Times Sunday Book Review* (5 September 2010), 16.

5. Uncredited, *Publishers Weekly*, https://www.publishersweekly.com/9781931520621.

6. John Taylor, *Paths to Contemporary French Literature*, vol. 1 (New Brunswick: Transaction, 2004), 220.

7. Jean-Luc Moreau, *La Nouvelle fiction* (Paris: Criterion, 1992), 208. My translation.

8. Moreau, *La Nouvelle fiction*, 201. My translation.

9. Taylor, *Paths to Contemporary French Literature*, 223.

10. Moreau, *La Nouvelle fiction*, 201. My translation.

The Messengers

Freilich, unwissend bin ich, die Wahrheit bleibt jedenfalls bestehn.
Certainly I am very ignorant, but nonetheless the truth exists.
FRANZ KAFKA

Gray overtakes the orchards to either side of the road. At times, through the mist, the first lights of a town flicker in the distance. Now and again, the youth comes upon a man on foot or a horse and cart making haste in the falling dark. Farmhouses grow more frequent: low-roofed in these lands, narrow-windowed, they look like large beasts belly-flat by the roadside beneath a great weight of sky—moles, hedgehogs, slugs, all things purblind and earthbound. Round a bend in the hedge hunches a serving girl, shivering with cold and quiet in the wind, who to watch the stranger pass opens wide her one good eye, the cloud on the other and the hump on her back the whole of her birthright. A tattered smock clothes her jutting bones. From atop the rise, she smiles as with one last step the youth draws abreast; another will sunder them forever, and suddenly, he no longer dares pass without a word. Night seems not to fall from above so much as seep from the trees and thin in the air like a cloud of ink in a glass of water.

"Good evening. Is it a long way to town?"

"I don't know. I think so."

"And this town . . . is it a big one?"

"So they say. I don't know."

Likely she knows little more than the paths to the well and the stables, having trodden them day after day. Her world is a fringe of field and pasture around the farmhouse courtyard, and the rest hearsay. The stranger points a finger at the roof behind her, among the trees.

"You live there?"

She turns, then nods. "Yes. And you?"

"Nowhere. I roam."

She nods again. She hasn't understood but won't insist. The boy shifts his weight from one foot to the other. He doesn't know what else to say, he thinks of moving on.

"Look—it's night now."

The two youths raise their heads. The sky is but a dark mass above, moonless, starless, with nowhere the barest glimmer to be seen. Three scant steps lie between them, yet scarcely can they see each other's faces through the pitch of night and fog. She takes his hand.

"Come, if you want."

"Where to?"

"Where it's warm, and you can eat . . . since you live nowhere."

Before he can say a word, she pulls him swiftly after her, down narrow footpaths where he stumbles and low branches lash him in passing. She is running, almost.

Tripping hard on a stump, he nearly falls, losing hold of the hand that guides him, and is suddenly scared.

"Hey! Hey, where'd you go?" He risks a step forward, arms outstretched in the dark. The hand takes hold of him again—his shoulder, this time—and he breathes a sigh of relief.

"This way! And don't make so much noise. No one must know."

"Why not?"

The hand slips down his arm, scrawny fingers tightening around his wrist. She pulls him along without reply. She's slowed her pace, for fear of losing him again. At last, the darkness clears before them. The boy makes out, arranged around a pyre in the middle of the courtyard, long tables laid with white cloth. Men in shirtsleeves, women in blouses despite the cool night air, bustle about garnishing these tables with platters, provisions, and pitchers, often pausing to sample wine or fare. Jests and laughter mingle with the crackle of the bonfire they feed. Two women reach deep into the wicker hamper they bear between them, scattering handfuls of flowers over dishes and tablecloth. There are musicians, too, flexing numb fingers over the fire. At their feet are glasses, bottles, musical instruments. One, more impatient than his fellows, starts his warm-up. An opening squeal of Breton bagpipes rises, harsh and reedy against the backdrop of voices.

"A celebration, is it? Let's have a look!"

The girl's fingers tense on his arm. Her mouth twists in anger, or fear. "No, no, you mustn't! Stay with me, it's better this way."

"But why not? Are they cruel? They don't look it . . ."

"They can be. Come. Come with me, I know a quiet place. Wait for me there, I'll bring you good things to eat, you'll see. Wine, and spirits, too, if I can. Come!"

These people, gathered so merrily round the fire—why would they do him any harm? He shrugs and follows the little hunchbacked girl, since she insists. By furtive bounds, fleeing the light pooled below the windows, stopping to catch their breath beneath a barrow in the U-shaped shadow of its long arms, they reach the far side of the courtyard, where the only unlighted barn stands back from the rest of the farm.

"In there?"

She pushes open the barn door, they fall into the close shadows.

"Give me your hand. We have to climb in the dark."

Things are strewn all over the floor, and he struggles; his floundering stirs odors of old hemp, straw and leather, rusted iron. He stifles a curse.

"Everything's here, old harnesses, tools, sacks. Instead of throwing them out, they put them here, right under where I live. A scrap of leather, a scrap of iron . . . who knows, they might come in handy? Careful—the step."

He follows her docilely up a stairwell that gives off a dusty smell of raw wood. They've passed the next floor, where apples and walnuts winter behind sealed windows. She draws him ever upward.

"It's way up top. The highest spot on the farm, that's where I live!"

At last they reach the loft. A faint glow from the courtyard's blaze dogears shadows round the window.

"Get down, for just a moment."

He complies, just long enough for her to cover the opening with a square of sackcloth. A match flares, hollowing a grotto of light from the darkness of the loft. She is seated on a straw mattress, a candle in her hands, a big box of kitchen matches half-spilled across her lap.

"Oh, how silly of me! Wait." She jams the candle in the neck of a green bottle already furred with soot and plucks the matches one by one from the folds of her smock. "Sit down. It's nice here, isn't it?"

Her eye, surveying the little she owns, gleams with quiet contentment, and the boy, a lump in his throat, says, "Yes, it's nice, it really is. It must be nice for you here."

"Oh yes, it is!" She leaps to her feet, grabs the candle, and brandishes it above her, casting light into the rafters. "Look! Nests . . . there, there, and there! Can you see?"

He says yes.

"And I've set traps for the rats. You mustn't touch them once they're set, or they'll suspect something."

She is breathless from speaking quickly, as lonely people do after too long a silence. She notices, laughs, apologizes. “Oh, I must be wearing you out with all my chatter! You stay here; I’ll go down and find us some food. I’ll be quick. You can lie down. It’s good ticking. Don’t show your head, don’t budge, all right?”

And she is gone, the words flung up from among slats of stairs through which he catches a last glimpse of her. The sound of her steps fades . . . he is alone. The straw crackles under his weight, he stretches out his weary legs. He mulls on the girl; perhaps, were she prettier, her eye unclouded, with curves besides the hump on her back and some color to her cheeks, she’d have let him walk on by earlier, little vagabond, too small a fry. But what does he know of girls? Nothing. Except the knowing looks from oft-eyed beauties, which leave him sheepish, arms dangling and legs leaden. But this girl? Harmless. And my, but taking her time . . . where is she? What if he took just a peek? With two spit-dampened fingers he snuffs the candle, then cautiously draws back the sackcloth. So much wood has been tossed on the fire that the scene is bright as day. Were every figure not coupled at the coat-tails with a shadowy giant on the beaten earth, no one would believe the late hour. The festivities have begun. Some feast, heedless of tables yet unset, and others dance with the febrile sprightliness of those hankering only to jig, while others still are already nattering on by the fire to anyone who will listen. No sooner do the musicians come together as a group than they scatter this way and that, one plopping down on the ground to play as he pleases, another clambering atop a barrel. Several go from table to table, freshening their feverish lips with a goblet of white wine quickly quaffed before drifting off, every man for himself but always on the beat despite the din. And there, off to the right, bearing a dish and bottles, the serving girl makes her way through the crowd. A matron must have pressed her into service. There she is now, at the head table. A tall man, head haloed in white hair, bids her come with a wave. She hurries over. He is the farmer, almost lordly here. Larger, heavier, more settled in himself than any man around, and everyone knows it. The girl freezes before him. He speaks. She sets his dish, his bottles, down on the table and takes off running down the path toward the main building. A long moment passes before she reappears. The master of the house leans forward, listening to the child's message. She utters a few words, then shrinks back three steps. Turning toward those assembled, the man raises an arm to command silence. All obey. Reeds leave lips, bows lift, voices and laughter grow hushed. The pewter goblet poised to land in ringing punctuation to a drunken argument settles softly, as though turned to glass, on the stained tablecloth. There is the final ruckus of a toppled chair across from the head table. Then nothing—no sound save the crackle of flames. A woman makes her way forward among the unmoving groups: alone, lifting with hands gloved to the elbow the hem of her austere dress. Her hair, in a jet-black band, frames only a mask of white tulle. She comes to the table, touches the man's hand. He rises and offers her a chair. Once seated, they exchange a few words. Still speaking, not even turning to acknowledge the watchful crowd, she breaks the spell with a mere wave of her hand. The guests resume eating and drinking, playing their instruments, dancing in a deafening tumult. From on high, the boy has eyes only for the regal couple. Even seated, the man is so tall he almost has to look down when a valet comes bearing a message. The woman herself, slender though she'd seemed while parting the crowd a moment earlier, looks like a little girl beside him. Not an inch of her skin can be seen, but she stirs in the boy more desire than any of the women who, blouses open to the waist and cheeks red with wine and merrymaking, nonchalantly hike up their skirts to itch themselves or flaunt their lace. And that face! He shivers just trying to picture it. Where a worldlier sort might envision revealings of another variety, the inventive naivete of the boy's age whispers for his imagination to draw aside the veil ever so slowly and gaze upon that forbidden visage. Down below, as the guests gorge themselves around her, she touches not a thing she has been served; nor has she, behind the tulle, wet her lips except from the man's cup, and that only barely. Meanwhile, after his initial ceremonious interest, the man has turned his attentions to his neighbor on the left, a parlor maid or sharecropper's daughter—how to tell? Cheek flushed, eye a-twinkle, she nonetheless dares not answer her master's cajolery too freely in the veiled woman's presence. Noticing this, the man gives his hindrance of a companion a look of displeasure. She leans forward then, and, it seems, takes her leave of him with a sigh. But she does not retire at once, awaiting instead a diversion to rise from the table without drawing attention. A segment of poorly propped-up pyre, collapsing in a spray of sparks, provides just that. Firebrands roll all the way to the tables. No one is hurt, but still, shouts ring out, exclamations. Someone seated too close to the flames plucks an ember from his plate, shows it around to much laughter. Already, two men are herding the logs back toward the fire with pitchforks. The seat to the master's right is empty. The music resumes, couples reconvene. The younger woman no longer fears the farmer's smile.

"Ho! I thought I told you—"

The youth gives a start. With everything going on in the courtyard, he didn't hear the cripple come back. "Oh, it's you. I was just looking. I saw you speak with the master."

"He told me to go fetch his lady. She came."

"And left again quite soon!"

The girl frowns. She crosses to the window and leans out over the courtyard. "Yes. Feast or no, it happens often. Light the candle again, would you? Here you are."

She hands him a bottle, a roll of bread, a trencher of meat. "As for apples and walnuts, we can have our fill!"

Side by side they sit on the straw mattress, each picking in turn at morsels of meat from the trencher. Soon the bottle is empty.

"You only brought one?"

"No, the other's at the foot of the stairs. I was afraid I'd spill it. Stay put, you'll fall."

She comes back with apples; walnuts, too. "Do you know how to crack them?"

He laughs. "Take two and squeeze them together: the weaker one breaks. Who d'you take me for?"

"I thought you might not know, since you're not from around here."

For a moment he suspects her of mockery—but no, in the candle's dancing flicker he spies no trace of irony in that unsightly little face. Is she even capable of such a thing? And why has she brought him here? The thoughts of too simple a soul lie in shadow. Oh, he'd been passing through, that's all. He fastens his mouth to the bottle's own and tosses his head back. When he sets the bottle down again, it is half-empty.

"That woman . . . she is beautiful!"

It is the girl's turn to drink. "Who's that? Oh, the lady of the house. Beautiful? For all we know. No one's ever laid eyes on her, not since the master brought her here. Maybe she's got no nose, or she has lupus, or she's cross-eyed! Or even one-eyed like me, but ashamed of it."

"Oh, no! Surely you're mistaken. She must be beautiful, the fairest of them all! And he treats her so poorly! But I'll be on my way now."

"Now? It's late. You can stay. It's a wide mattress."

"Thank you. You're kind, but I must go."

"You can stay. Even if you don't want me—it's no matter."

The boy blushes, looks away. "What do you mean?"

"You know very well. But it's no matter. You can stretch out and sleep here, if you want."

In a trice she's cleared aside the trencher, dusted the mattress free of crumbs and nutshells. He rises to finish the bottle and totters; all that wine has gone to his head. But he perseveres and drains it to the dregs. The girl has taken a few steps back, outside the circle of light.

"Turn around."

He does as told. A rustle of cloth from behind vaguely stirs his drunken elation. He turns. At first the girl makes as if to wave him off and then, with a shrug, slips out of her last layer and goes back to the mattress, where she pulls the blanket over her. He catches a glimpse of a slight, pale frame, all crooked, smudged with shadow below the belly. Something shifts in his chest; he isn't sure if he wants to touch her body or brush her cheek, wipe away unseen tears with a comradely hand as if she's wounded herself in some lasting way. He sits down beside her, his hand reaching to pull the blanket away. She speaks then, in a whisper without a trace of anger.

"No, leave me be. You don't want to. You're considering it, but deep down, you don't want to."

She blows out the candle. A red dot hisses for a few seconds, the smell of burnt wick spreading. He sits there, lost in his uncertain thoughts. After a while, the sound of the serving girl's breathing grows more regular. She is asleep. He rises, does his best to find his bearings, and finally gropes his way to the stairs. One flight down, he wanders the maze of pungent wicker racks before finding his way to the ground floor. Outside, the collapsed pyre tosses final flickers of red at the windows. It has all been left to the night: tables littered with platters and soiled napkins, dishes congealing in their sauces, flowers drowned in wine from toppled pitchers. Everywhere, derelict instruments slumber on chairs, lean on table corners, or simply lie forgotten on the ground like strange, bulging insects bristling with antennae. Men and women ambushed by sleep snore away beneath tables, across joined chairs, where fatigue overtook them. A drunkard with a wrinkled brow, seated before a violin, timidly picks out a few moony pizzicato notes in the night. The youth hesitates. But he thirsts. He pours himself one glass, then another. A wan face shows in a doorway and vanishes as quickly as it came, expunged by the night. No one pays the youth any mind. He gives over glass and pitcher for a handier bottle and sets out to explore the wide-open buildings. Everywhere, upon stepping over the doorsill, he is greeted by the same concert of snores, groans, muddled interjections. He presses on. The floorboards alone wake at his steps. Trailing fingers over furniture, curios, ancestral portraits, he goes, silently pushing past doors, up flights of stairs, down hallways;

the farm stretches, swells, sprawls, and still he goes, surreptitious inspector of stupors and respirations, seeking he knows not what. At the sound of footsteps coming toward him from around a corner his ears prick up. He ducks into the first room at hand, not daring to shut the door for fear the click of the latch might rouse the recumbent figure he finds there from a slumber troubled by unintelligible entreaties. Through the crack in the door, he sees a circle of light grow and brighten the corridor as the footsteps draw closer. He holds his breath. It is a black woman of boundless beauty. Her features belie the darkness of her skin, betraying mixed origins: straight nose, fine lips, hair falling in soft braids on her chest. She wears a long nightgown and, in her left hand, holds a three-armed candelabrum with two candles, only one lighted. Her right hand clutches a fistful of fabric at her hip to keep her lace hem from the dusty floorboards. Her face is suffused with melancholy. The youth caught but a glimpse of her from where he hides, yet though already the corridor dims and the sound of her footsteps fades away, every detail of her appearance remains graven in his memory. Scorning all caution, he steps out from hiding. The woman has vanished round another corner of the corridor. The boy gives chase. The hallway leads to a stairwell he didn't notice in passing, its steps carpeted in crimson. She climbs them without pause. Heart beating, temples buzzing, he follows suit. They emerge onto a narrow landing, mere yards apart. Rather than muffling sounds, the crimson rug seems louder than the floorboards below, but the woman does not turn. Perhaps she mistakes the youth's footfalls for her own, however light and nearly inaudible? At the end of this new hallway stands a closed door. The sight of this dead end gives the youth pause. Were the woman to turn around, they would find themselves face to face. Already she has covered more than half the distance from the stairwell to the door. He flouts his fears. She stops in front of the door. He does the same. For a long while they stay that way, unmoving. No doubt the woman, troubled by what she fears to behold, struggles to quell the pounding of her heart. At last her right hand reaches out; with a creak, the door swings open. The youth has moved closer. He is now but three steps from the woman, already breathing her scent. Like hers, his gaze searches the shadows of the room. She lifts the candlestick to see better. In the middle of the room, on a mussed bed, two bodies lie intertwined. The white-haired farmer sleeps on his back, mouth open. The younger woman—the same one who smiled at him earlier that evening at the table—is pressed to him in surrender. The boy reels. An unfamiliar odor rises from the sleeping couple, mingling with the woman's perfume, making his head spin. A muscle in her dark shoulder twitches under the fabric. She is pushing the door shut. Next she will turn and see him standing there. He takes a step toward her, blows out the only candle. A brief cry, and then all is silence. Nimbly, he flattens himself against the wall. A hand, feeling its way along, brushes him; he dodges it. The woman moves farther away. Her steps, tentative at first, recover their sureness. A draft must have blown out the candle as she shut the door. The boy waits before following her again. Not until she has reached the foot of the stairs does she quite recover from her fright and give a thought to relighting the candle. Briefly she lifts the candelabrum toward the steps she's just descended. The boy remains huddled in the gloom, spying on her dark face where soon nothing can be read beyond a trace of unease but great sadness. They set out again, the mulattress with her usual stride, majestic despite herself, and he almost darting on tiptoe from nook to cranny. Stairwells, hallways, come one after another. The youth lets himself be led along. He has done so much walking, gone up and down so many steps, turned and veered right and left, that he long ago lost all notion of bearings and could never have found his way back to the world outside. At long last, they reach the foot of a final staircase, this one carpeted in black. They ascend. Upstairs, at the end of a hallway, a door stands ajar. The woman goes through. A ray of light leaks out from under the door. Slowly, the boy approaches; each step costs him. More than once, he recoils, struck by the absurdity of his actions; nothing is possible, nothing permitted. She will scream, he'll be hunted down, perhaps even killed. But if, moved by his youth, she should welcome him without making a scene? What would he say to her, what does he want from her? Even should she consent—the act of love, he wouldn't know, couldn't even begin to . . . Naturally, the body he's made out beneath the nightgown has roused in him the same turmoil he's sometimes felt upon catching women bathing naked by the river's edge, or seeing the serving girl earlier. They weren't all beautiful, those women, but his blood had always throbbed faster in his veins. But that feeling can't be all there is! What next, then? He panics, shuffles in place, dares neither to advance nor retreat, panting. All the shuffling has worn him out more than a league at full sprint. The bottle he hasn't relinquished during all his wanderings weighs abruptly heavy at the end of his arm. He brings it to his lips and drains it. At first, nausea; then the wine's warmth comforts him. Along the bottom of the door, the line of light has thinned. No doubt the woman has moved the candelabrum. A moment later, all is dark. The night, abetted by the wine, emboldens him. His hand falls on the knob. He enters without violence, a fluid movement none could fear. Stagnant at the window as rainwater in a wheel rut, what light is left from the courtyard bonfire reveals the room without truly illumining it. Beneath the casement, a dresser top surfacing from shadow. Linen lies balled there, still soft from warm flesh. To the right, a bed. Where a figure has just sat up. In the time it takes his vision to adjust, the youth makes out the shape of a face against the paler night of the sheets. Alarmed, a voice rises in the dark.

"Who's there?"

The boy speaks. He strains his voice, to hide its humiliating quaver. "Forgive me, milady."

"Who are you? What is this?"

"Nothing, milady. I . . ." All courage deserts him. He kneels beside the woman's bed and hides his face in his hands. "I am a stranger, a drifter just passing through. I wanted to tell you . . . I saw everything down there, in the room at the end of the red-carpeted hall. I was behind you!"

The woman stiffens. Her fear is gone now, but her voice takes on a distant tone that heightens the child's embarrassment. "And?"

"And—and . . . I don't know, milady. I followed you. I wanted to tell you . . ."

"What is it you wished to tell me?"

"That you are beautiful—so beautiful! Oh, I don't understand anything that goes on here, I don't even know who you are, I don't know anyone—not master or mistress, the lady in the veil, or the young woman sleeping with the master downstairs. I know no one but the little hunchbacked serving girl . . ."

"It is time I saw you!" The woman strikes the tinder and holds the flame toward his face. "How young you are! Why—you're crying! Have you no home, poor child? And have you truly no idea who I am?"

"You are so beautiful!"

"And you are sweet. You do know that, don't you? I am but a poor soul. Go now. Better you should not know who I am."

The candelabrum is there, on the nightstand. She lights the tapers in two of its arms. In their glow, she has a thought for her nakedness, and covers her breast.

"Stop staring!"

He looks down, blushing. Then raises his head again and speaks abruptly, a man's bitterness in his voice. "Why not? I wish to look upon you! I don't know how to tell you. You're too beautiful!"

The woman laughs, drawing the sheets up higher.

"Come now, be a good boy! I belong to a man."

The boy's face is nothing now but suffering. "That much I understood. You belong to the master. But he belongs to no one! Not to his wife, who must also be so beautiful beneath that mask, nor the other young woman, nor you, nor anyone else."

The woman frowns. "You were so sweet, till now. Why say such wicked things to me?"

"I didn't mean to! I love you! Oh, you can't even know! I was going on my way, not asking anything of anyone, not a halfpenny or a crust of bread, I wasn't unhappy, it seemed the road before me would never end . . . And then the serving girl led me here. I should never have followed her, I know that now, I did a bad thing, something has broken. Never again will the dawn be as it once was, plain and bright . . . I love you, and I love him, too—the master! I love him despite myself! Oh, I feel sick to my stomach, I've had too much to drink. I shouldn't say another word, but I can't help it, I just keep talking and talking, I feel like I'll go on talking forever now, until I die: only a mouthful of earth will deliver me. It's filthy, it's wrong! The master, I don't know what it is I feel when I look at him. Sometimes I want to hit him, hurt him, burn his farm down, poison his livestock, soil his bed, steal his women . . . And then, other times, the desire to serve him, to please him sweeps over me, to bring a smile, a rimple of approval to his face no matter the cost. I would be his valet, I would saddle his horse; he would take me hunting with him, and I would carry his rifle . . . No, that's not it, I don't feel one way first and then the other, it's everything all at once, at the same time! And he's never even laid eyes on me . . . Oh, but I am mad!"

The child sobs beside the bed. The woman pulls him to her, gently. He goes to her, surrenders, buries his eyes, his face, in the fragrant hollow of her armpit.

"Mad, yes, a madman indeed, for he has no need of you. He needs no one, save perhaps a woman now and then, he cares little which. So think no more of it, be on your way tomorrow, or even at once. There is nothing for you here, believe me—nothing. You are no woman, fit to please him; no horse he might relish breaking in; not even a round pebble he might see fit to send rolling down the hill upon stepping out to greet the day. Away with you! Go, make a place for yourself elsewhere, live somewhere else, die somewhere else! No one here cares . . ."

"But you—if you wanted . . ."

The woman pulls away, worried. As she spoke, the scent of her skin, the nearness of her body, had gone to the child's head. His eyes glitter with a harder flame in a face still bathed in tears.

"There is nothing I want. Not a thing, do you hear?"

"Yes, oh yes! Please let me, please—I'll die if I can't!"

With a swift jerk, he tears the sheet aside. Brown flesh gleams in the glow from near tapers.

"Stop! Stop it! Leave this place. At once, or I'll call out!"

He begs, eyes straining from their sockets, hand clutching the sheet. The candle flames quiver, the air unsettled by the brusqueness of their movements.

"No, please don't call out, let me touch you, let me hold you, you're so beautiful, so—" His pleas turn to stammers. He wants to die, to hurl himself at this body as if at an abyss from atop a cliff, and fall, tumble, tumble endlessly, eyes open wide to the sky. The woman pushes him away firmly, but without anger; she does not want to scream.

"Stop, you poor fool! I fear for your sake. Calm yourself, I beg of you, and be gone. If I call them, they will kill you."

"Then don't call them, or do—I don't care!"

His hand tightens on the arm that guards her. He tugs, but the woman is strong. After resisting for a moment, she feigns surrender, quickly twists free, and in the same motion, slaps him. A rush of humiliation mingles with his burgeoning resentment. He rises up, straddles her, pressing all his weight against her. His hand fumbles at his belt.

"Fool! Fool! You are lost!"

She screams; the night comes flooding back. The youth brings his hands to his ears. The scream has pierced his head and slowly, ever so slowly, begins boring its way deeper, an auger. When he bursts, there will be nothing left of him but a flaccid sheath, boneless, strengthless, in the hands of the mob. They will take him by the foot and drag him—helpless, a sundered puppet—to the dung-heap, there to rot in the waste of man and beast, among the maggots. The woman has pulled the sheet back over her. He's opened his eyes; he sees her through a fog. He lowers his hands; the right is stained with blood. Her nails must have raked his cheek. She speaks now in an urgent whisper.

"Go now, will you be gone! They're on their way, they will hurt you. Quick—quick, before I scream again!"

Hastily he straightens his clothes, gets to his feet, stumbles into the furniture. His hand falls on a scrap of cloth. He presses it to his cheek to stanch the blood. Voices, the sounds of doors and footsteps begin ringing out through the house.

One last time, the woman exhorts: "Flee!"

Her mouth opens. She howls. He runs from the room, pushes past a shadow in the hallway, tears down the stairs, turns down another hallway. Doors open in his wake, arms reaching, exclamations ring out, oaths. He makes his way through a forest of hands, fearsome faces. Men growl, terrified women shriek. He runs, one hand on his half-buttoned pants that threaten with each step to fall to his ankles. A man surges from round a corner and grabs him. The boy roars, bites, scratches, lashes out with feet and fists, finally breaks free. The manor is nothing now but colossal cacophony. On every side, people are waking, calling out to one another, reaching for weapons. Just as he is about to lose hope, he bursts into the fresh air, abruptly face to face with the pyre's embers. In the courtyard, they are already shaking off sleep, windows opening in the neighboring buildings. From the kennel rises the baying of hounds. He crosses the courtyard and freezes for a moment by the serving girl's barn. Someone calls out to him in a whisper. He gives a start. It's her. She pulls him into the shadows.

"Good Lord, what have you done, what have you done? And just look at you!"

He looks down, hides his shame.

"I can guess. And now they're after you. I warned you, didn't I?"

He's done buttoning himself up now. He spreads his arms in hapless apology. It wasn't his fault; it all happened despite himself.

"You must flee. Look!"

She points toward the courtyard. Able-bodied men have gathered. They're bringing the dogs now, weapons are being passed around—pitchforks, cudgels, a few hunting rifles. The white-haired man, fiercer and more furious than the rest, issues orders to his little army: catch the prowler, dead or alive! The youth glances at the windows, where women are leaning out. The mulattress is not among them. But he seems to glimpse, higher up, surrounded by chambermaids, a woman in a veil. The hunchback pinches his arm.

"Snap out of it, dolt! You're the one they're after! Come with me!"

She pushes the door open, grabs his hand, and just as when they first met, leads him among the old things strewn across the dirt floor to the far wall.

"Luckily, there's a way out here. Help me. Push."

She's lifted the bar from a sealed-up window. The shutters creak on their rusted hinges. Cool air bathes his face. On this side, far from the pyre, the night is starless, dark as can be desired.

"Head straight through the fields. You've a chance at escape if you run fast. Go, and be well!"

She helps him clamber over the windowsill.

Once over, he falls to the ground, scrabbling in the slick loam. At the window, the girl is losing her patience. He stands up.

"Thank you."

"Run!"

He can see nothing. The darkness around him is complete. He cannot even make out his own hands. Left, right, dogs bark, men shout. He plunges straight ahead into the night. He bolts blindly, crashes into fences, trees, haystacks, trips on every mound of dirt, twists his ankle in furrows, collapses, keeps going, falls again, knees skinned, hands bloodied, mops himself now and then with the cloth he grabbed from the woman's bedroom, now but a scrap stained with sweat-thinned blood and mud. Two lines of torches light the countryside behind him. His pursuers have split into two groups. They move swiftly, see clearly; the dogs bark. He sets out again, hurls himself into a stream, fords it, whimpering with cold and fright, falls and gets back up again ten times over. He runs for a long, long time. Night draws to a close, the sky pales at the horizon. Bit by bit, the barking grows more distant. He still seems to hear it, though, and the roars of the men, but it is just the pounding of his heart, the swish of frigid air in his throat, his ragged lungs. He slows down. No, he can't hear a thing anymore, now. He has run till it is day; he can go no further. All around him, the world is coming into being: hedges, trees piercing the dawn mists. The land is ashiver with morning vapor. He walks stiffly, taking little steps like an old man. Then, under a tree in the middle of a field, he lies down and vomits harshly, long wine-colored spurts, before falling asleep. Slowly, the earth warms. The sun climbs in the sky. The verdure murmurs with chirruping sparrows.

A magpie falls like a stone, gives a shake, and hops about, strutting amid clumps of sod. Swiftly the shrew scarpers into its hole. The sun is in the middle of the sky when a peasant woman in a black smock passes by along the field's edge, wooden clogs smacking the dirt, without seeing the boy. He keeps sleeping, nose in his vomit. Much later, the same steps sound again on the gravel path. This time, the peasant woman sees him. She brushes a lock of gray hair from her forehead and approaches, bowed over her walking stick.

"Well, well! Must've been quite the carousing! Ho, you! Sleepyhead! Hear me?"

He opens one eye. The terrors of the night, the long chase, it all comes rushing back through his stupor. He panics, his hands rise to his face to shield it. The old woman shrinks back.

"Oh! I mean you no harm! It's no crime, sleeping in a field . . . it's not even my field! Don't get all worked up!"

Seeing she is alone and old reassures him. He speaks with difficulty; his furred tongue feels clumsy. "You startled me!"

"I can tell! You leapt like a man at the sound of guards coming to drag him to the scaffold! Say, you've been on quite the tear. You reek like nobody's business!"

The purplish stain emits a foul stench. He rolls aside, moves away, but the odor is coming from him, his sullied shirt, his very flesh, it seems. He strips the shirt off and flings it as far as he can. The stench persists. His cheek, the nape of his neck, his hands are spattered with ordure. Nausea doubles him over.

"And so young! You're off to a bad start, my boy, a bad start. I've seen your sort, all sweetness and light, and then—off on a spree! If you could see them now . . ."

He stands up as best he can, leaning on the tree. "Everything's spinning . . . I feel awful!"

The old woman snickers. "That'll learn you! Hah! What did you think would happen? You had too much to drink, that's all! Here, have some of this."

She holds out a canteen. He opens it, takes a sniff, goes pale. It is brimming with red wine.

"No, no, go on, drink. It's the only way. Now, if you want to stay sick like this all day, well, that's up to you. Afterwards, you'll need food. Here, I might have a little snack left over. At my age, you just don't get that hungry anymore. Here, take it."

He eats, drinks because she tells him to. He also wants to wash up. "Is there a well nearby, where I can clean up?"

"Yes, yes, I'll show you. It's on my way. Meanwhile, eat. Drink."

He does his utmost to chew despite his disgust. He's feeling a bit better, but still—that stench!

"Well, come along now. Oh, you've left your handkerchief there on the ground."

He bends over. It's the rag from the woman's room. He's hung onto it the whole way. He shrugs.

The old woman exclaims, "Don't tell me you're just leaving that there! It can be washed, you know. Let me see!"

She examines the pitiful thing. "Say, this isn't a handkerchief, it's lace—and fine lace at that! A veil, it looks like. Don't toss it aside, it must be worth money. You should wash it."

The youth, who has already turned to go, freezes, thoughtful. He shivers, shirtless in the tree's shade. "No, it's ruined. Might as well throw it out."

The old woman turns the soiled fabric this way and that, poking her fingernail at spots caked with mud and vomit. "Where'd you get this, anyway? Why, there's even blood on it. Oh, right, from your cheek. Some pretty little thing playing hard to get, eh? She sure got you good, didn't she? Ah, that's how girls are. Well, it's no matter no mind to me. But if you don't want it anymore, I'll take it."

"All right. It's yours. But can we go now? I want to wash up. I stink!"

They walk side by side. Sometimes he stumbles; his stiff legs pain him, but he forces himself, in a hurry. The old woman scurries along, the unspeakable little veil in hand. They fall silent. The way to the well is long.

"Here we are. Toss the bucket in."

The winch creaks in the silence. The bucket comes up, full of frigid water. He dunks his head in, splashes his chest and back, scrubs his skin as hard as he can. Beside him, the old woman cackles, alarmed by the spray he sends flying every which way.

"Ho! Careful now, it's not my bath day! I'm not the one who reeks of cheap wine. I don't need a soaking!"

Done, he lies down in the sun to dry. The old woman hoists up another bucket of water, plunges the veil in, scrubs it, and wrings it out carefully before spreading it flat on a stone.

"There. That'll do for the worst of it. I'll get the rest back home, with soap." She takes a peek to make sure he hasn't changed his mind now that the veil is clean. He hasn't budged. He keeps his eyes closed, resting.

"Say, come to think of it, the mistress of that big farm back there wears little veils like these. Why, no one's ever seen her without one. That's not where you picked this up, is it? You must've passed by there on your way, eh? The prettiest of farms, there's no missing it, and her the prettiest of women, too. Her figure, at least—only her husband's ever seen her face, and even then, well, we do wonder, don't we; she's so particular about it, so they say. But if you've met her, maybe you got a peek at her without her veil, eh? Eh? You can tell me, I won't go blabbing it about. So did you see her? What's she like? What's she hiding? Go on, tell!"

The boy makes no reply. He feigns sleep, but the old woman isn't fooled. She pokes his arm with the end of her stick. "Ho! Asleep, are you? Can you hear me? Oh, I know full well you can. I saw you. I saw your eyelid flutter, I just know it, so why the act? I'm right on the money, aren't I? That veil is hers, I'd bet my life on it! Something must've happened. You took her, or tried to at least, and she fought back, but you came away with the veil, which means you must've seen her face!"

He sits up, gives her a dark look. "No, no, you've got it all wrong, that's not the way I came. I never ran into anyone. That veil, I . . . I found it, that's all. Leave me alone, will you? I've been walking all night, I'm exhausted. Thank you for the snack. Now, will you please leave me alone?"

"Don't want to talk about it, eh? Suit yourself. But I know what I think, and you can't stop me from thinking it, oh no! I know what I think, and that's all there is to it! For starters, we've had our doubts about her. Maybe she's not the one who left you in that state, maybe she even let you have your way with her, eh? And then someone else chanced unexpectedly upon the two of you! But you managed to get away with the veil all the same, something to remember that pretty little minx by! So that's what she does, eh? Spreads her legs for any young clodhopper who comes by! Well, that's no surprise to me. What's she hiding? Why, what's she got to hide? A woman with a figure like hers, keeping it all under wraps—that's not normal. She never shows so much as an inch of skin, not her hands, not even her feet—nothing!"

"Shut up! Leave me alone! I was never there, I'm telling you. I just found the veil on the ground . . ."

"So you say. But let me tell you something: the man who owns that farm? If you stole his wife away, he'll kill you, that's for sure—kill you!"

The youth leaps to his feet. He shouts, waves his arms at the old woman, his face pale with anger and fear. "Shut up, shut up! I didn't do anything wrong, I don't even know her, or him, I don't know anyone over there!"

The old woman shouts right back. Her squeals must carry a mile off. "My eye you didn't! You had that little tart! You had her, and that's the truth! Don't go spinning yarns with me, you little brat! Oh, he'll kill you, do you hear? That man'll kill you, and how! He'll snap your neck like you're a rat caught nibbling the grain."

Abruptly, the old woman falls silent. She takes a step back. Something in the boy's bearing has unsettled her. He's not shouting anymore, there's nothing on his face now but boredom, and still he comes closer, arms folded over his belly. She wants to be on her way. After all, this is no matter no mind of hers. She's just a poor, doddering old woman, she mustn't be blamed. Her tongue tends to wag, too much maybe, many's the time they've told her and she knows it, but she has a good heart, that much can't be denied. From the corner of her eye, she casts furtively about for her walking stick, but it's too late. The boy is upon her, grabbing her with both hands. She screams. No time to put up a fight; a few quick steps of a grotesque *pas de deux* and they're at the well. He throws her in headfirst, in a dusty blossoming of underthings. A dull smack, a distant slosh, and it's done. A silence like a startled blackbird's falls over the land. The boy puts on his wet shirt, unhurried. It'll dry on him; the sun is yet high in the sky. The old woman's walking stick still lies in the grass. He picks it up, tosses it at the well. His aim is true; he grins. He bends over, gathers the damp veil, and presses it to his forehead at first to shield him from the sun, but it's awkward. He walks back to the well, flings it in, watches it fall. The well is deep, the shadows are thick. The scrap of lace, soon swallowed up, disappears. Unaccustomed emotion overcomes him. The sky is blazing, the stone rim has reopened the scratches on his knees. The pulley wheel creaks. The youth sways over the abyss with its fresh scent of water and stone. The well received the offering. The wind, no doubt, tearing white petals from a sapling . . . The drifter steps back down from the well's edge. He takes his bearings from the sun, which set the day before on a distant town. He sets off toward it, taking great strides. He walks for a long time. As he climbs from a dell, he makes out a road to the right, between two stands of trees—the very one he'd been on yesterday. Instead of heading for it, he opts to cut straight on through the countryside, keeping the road in sight as much to avoid the meanders imposed by terrain as the suspicions of passersby who might have caught wind of the scandal and last night's manhunt. The afternoon is drawing to a close. The youth shivers in his damp shirt. He hastens his step, crosses a field, hurdles a hedge, and reaches the edge of a river, its waters slow and gray. Ahead, the road ends in a bridge that failed when the river last flooded—some time ago, to judge by the weeds overrunning its wreckage. Downstream, a fragile footbridge has been tossed across the river, a makeshift lashing of rope and plank that shakes and shrieks at the slightest gust. Likely a broader bridge a few miles upstream, or even a ferry, caters to carriage traffic. Travelers on foot disheartened by the dizzying footbridge must press on for it as well. The spot is deserted, save for the figure of a man on the far bank, almost directly across from the boy. Both he and the youth walk, on their separate shores, toward the footbridge. The man is tall, stooped. Long silver locks of hair flutter disarrayed beneath the brim of his hat. His trappings, of a cut that might from a distance pass for stylish—halfway between a ranking official's formal dress (but with neither badge nor braid) and a burgher's evening wear—hang, upon closer inspection, in shapeless folds on his scrawny frame. The vagaries of the riverside path—now straying from the shore to lose its way among trees for a spell, now returning to run close by the line of gray water—alternately hide and reveal the man. A day laborer's beige haversack bounces at the small of his back, an unexpected sight against the black cloth. He walks head down, never sparing a glance at the other shore. If he's seen the boy, he does not show it. In unison, they lean into the sharp slope leading up to the footbridge. As he climbs, the youth weighs in his mind whether to slow and let the man take the bridge first, or instead quicken his step and forge ahead without waiting. Before he can make up his mind, they reach the top at the same time. He pauses on the cusp of the bridge. As for the man, he seems in no hurry to cross. He sits himself down on the grassy embankment, a few steps from the footbridge. He does not move. The youth hesitates. An infernal wind roars through these heights, the void yawns; a hundred feet below, dark waters roil. The rope thrums in his hand. The planks knock and clatter, thin strips of wood strung devil-may-care from the guy ropes, unevenly spaced, perhaps even rotted. On the far bank, the man in black is still seated. He's slipped his haversack off his shoulder and onto his lap. With his gaze, he follows the tethers' ceaseless swaying. The youth clears his throat before calling out over the howl of the wind and creaking of the footbridge.

"Ho, there! Sir! Hello!"

The man looks up—without haste, and without reply at first, almost regretfully.

"Hey! If you want to cross, go ahead! I said, if you want to cross, go ahead! I'll wait!"

"No, no, cross if you want, boy. I'm not headed that way."

"Oh. But I thought . . ."

Already the man's thoughts are elsewhere. He looks down again, fiddling with who knows what deep in his haversack. Despite the spinning in his head, the boy takes another few steps forward.

"All right, coming through! It sure is high! And swinging a lot, huh?"

"Come." The man's voice is but a whisper. He makes a vague wave that could mean anything—*come, don't, I don't care* . . . Perhaps in the end he never said a thing, or he was thinking of something else; perhaps it was but a whim of the wind, mimicking the sound of a human voice on the outflung cords. The man has closed his haversack again. He looks up, casually following the boy's quaking progress over the abyss, sometimes turning to gaze at the gloomy sky, the trees, the grass at his feet. He plucks a blade of grass, brings it to his mouth. He's enjoying his little rest after climbing the promontory. On the footbridge, the wind howls; life is vertigo, a nauseous progress over the void. The planks slip from underfoot, the rope gives way with weight, twisting and turning, fights when pulled, yields when pushed, jolting and jerking. The boy advances one step at a time, sweat on his brow, stomach heaving. He dares not turn back beneath the stranger's gaze. Then it's too late. Halfway across and deep in the heart of the tumult, turning around would cost him more than taking the next step. He pushes on, not entirely in control of his wobbly legs, hands ready to open, to let everything go for a great tumbling plummet; the promontory dances before his eyes. The man, stretched out, chews his blade of grass. The youth is very close now, but a final gust more violent than before hurls him from the path of planks. His hands knot around the ropes, his legs whip at the air above the rocky shore, he cries for help. The man does not move. The boy makes the last three feet on the strength of his arms alone, pulls himself up, then collapses in the grass, drenched in sweat. Beside him the man chews on, indifferent, gazing off into the distance. The youth's wrath explodes.

"I called out to you, and you didn't do a thing. You didn't even budge! How hard would it have been for you to reach out a hand? I could've died!"

The man stares at him. His gaze, between white locks the wind ruffles over his brow, is glacial. "Why would I have done such a thing?"

"Why . . . to help me! I was about to fall. To smash into those rocks!"

"Yes, yes, I know. I saw you. But why would I lift a finger to keep you from dying?"

The youth falls silent, dumbfounded by the man's cynicism. He has risen. He settles the haversack into the small of his back and tugs on the strap, tightening it against him. The youth rises in turn. Now they stand face to face.

“Well? Why? No answer? Run along now. Don’t go looking for trouble. It’s all the same to me, whether you live or die.”

He turns his back, and the boy leaps at him, fist raised. But he’s not fast enough. The man spins around, fends off the blow, lands his own to the boy’s stomach, then slaps him twice across the face. In the same instant, he grabs the boy by the scruff of the neck and now drags him to the very edge of the promontory, right by the footbridge. The boy begs, in tears. His nose is bleeding; he struggles to breathe. The man holds him over the abyss headfirst, shaking him roughly. Yet the man’s face bears no trace of anger. The brief scuffle has, at best, winded him slightly.

“And now? What do you say now, eh? I could toss you off right here, boy. Understand? Into the void!”

“No! No, you wouldn’t—”

“Oh, you think so, eh? And why wouldn’t I? I’ve got a reason to. And what is that? Say it!”

“B-because . . . because I jumped you.”

“There! You see? I’ve got good reason to toss you off this cliff. What am I going to do, in your opinion? Answer me!”

“I don’t know! I don’t know!” The youth weeps, short anxious sobs, in the man’s grip. For a few moments longer the man keeps him there, their faces uncomfortably close, then sends him rolling safe and sound into the tall grass.

"Aren't you going to thank me? You owe me your life now. Isn't that what you wanted, just a few minutes ago?"

The boy whimpers, head in his hands. "Yes, yes, thank you, thank . . ."

But the man isn't listening. He's already off, haversack slapping at the small of his back. He vanishes from view.

"Thank you! Oh, thank you!"

The boy weeps and whimpers a long while as night floods the promontory. Then, slowly, his nerves settle, his breathing calms, the sobs grow fewer and farther between. He stays there, prostrate, gnawing at his lip. The chill of night on his shoulders finally prompts him to rise. The footbridge is lost to evening mists. Nothing of the far bank can now be seen but the tips of the tallest trees, and even these soon fade, vanish into the gray. The great wind has quieted. A light breeze dries the last tears from the corners of his eyes. He races, sniffling, down the slope to the shore. At the river's edge, he presses his face into palmfuls of water, washes crusts of dried blood from his nose. He goes on his way, rejoins the road where it peels away toward the washed-out bridge. He walks quickly; he is cold and hungry. He scans the houses, ever closer together, for the wooden sign of an inn where a copper dredged up from deep in a pocket might buy him a bowl of soup. He's reached the outskirts of town. He loses his way wandering down poorly paved streets lined with factories, warehouses, vacant lots, shacks where, through many a window with only a smudge of grease and dust for a curtain, bickering families can be made out gathered round barren tables. All of a sudden he freezes, ducking into a doorway. There stands the man from the promontory, some fifty feet away in the middle of the street, beside a fiacre. He is speaking to the coachman. Across the way, an open café—the only one on the street, perhaps the neighborhood—shines in the night. The youth suppresses his impatience. He deems it wiser not to show himself. But the man lingers. He must be telling jokes; the coachman's laughter rings out. Will they never leave? Time passes; the café is closing. The boy's stomach torments him with cramps. Though still talking, the man has moved. His back is now turned to the café. Tired of twiddling his thumbs in the doorway, the youth dashes out onto the sidewalk. He crosses the street, pushes open the door. A paunchy man turns him away.

"Oh, no you don't! We're closed. Do you have any idea what time it is? Really, some people!"

"Just another minute, please! I'm so hungry! Let me wolf something down, and I'll be on my way, I promise!"

"Not my problem. It's closing time, so we're closing!"

The door slams, the bolt slides. The youth turns back to the street. The spat has drawn the two men's attention. Seeing nothing of interest, the coachman tries to keep the chitchat going, but the man in black silences him with a wave of his hand. He has recognized the boy. He crosses the street toward him.

"Is that you, boy? What are you doing here?"

The boy trembles in every limb. He shrinks back, pressing himself against the door. The man grows impatient.

"Well? Are you going to answer?"

"I was just passing by. I tried to go in. I was hungry. I wasn't following you, I swear, I was just passing by, that's all!"

The man says nothing. He seems lost in thought.

"And now, if you please, I'll just be on my way—"

"No. And stop acting like a dog with his tail between his legs. I won't hit you again. Tell me something: do you know where you're going?"

"No, sir, no, I have no idea. But if you let me go, I'll find another café, and somewhere to sleep."

"Really? You don't know anyone in this town?"

"No one, sir. I don't know anyone anywhere. But I'll manage. I'm used to it."

"You'll manage, eh? Where are you from, anyway? What do you do in life?"

The youth regains some of his courage. The man won't hit him anymore—he's said so, hasn't he? His voice grows stronger. He straightens up. "Oh, this and that. I wander, I drift here and there. I live by begging, pilfering, sometimes I do the odd job. I'm from . . . back thataway."

With his finger, he points vaguely in the direction of the countryside, the river.

"I know. But before that?"

"Before that, too. Things were the same back that-away, always have been, just farther off."

"But where are you going? Is someone waiting for you?"

"No, sir, no one, anywhere. I roam for my own pleasure, I guess . . ."

The man bursts out laughing. "For your own pleasure? You miserable boy! Do you mean that things are going well for you? Life is good?"

The boy looks down, upset. "I don't know. You ask hard questions! I'm not unhappy—not always. Or happy, of course. Sometimes I go hungry. But I don't know, I've never asked myself that question. That's how things are. It must be normal."

The coachman, who has said nothing till now, taps his foot impatiently. Without turning, the man calls over his shoulder, "Just a minute."

To the boy, he says, "You're coming with me."

"With you? Where?"

"You'll see. At least you'll eat your fill tonight. Well, what are you waiting for? Come, I say!"

These last few words are a growl. The boy obeys. The coachman has opened the door. They take their seats inside the fiacre. The coachman slams the door shut and clambers up into his seat. They start moving. One after another, streets go by, all penurious at first. Rats in the roadway, many and bold, barely deign to scamper aside and let the fiacre pass. Wan prowlers stalk the streets with slow strides. Painted women, stationed here and there on sidewalks, smoke cigarettes. But as the fiacre approaches the center of town, the gas lamps grow more frequent, shining more brightly over broader, better cared-for sidewalks. The streets widen too, becoming boulevards, avenues planted with chestnut trees. The paving improves, more level now. The fiacre rolls smoothly, silently along. Residences on either side of the avenue rise high into the dark sky, perforated by broad, bright bay windows. Fiacres are parked beside elaborate entranceways. They have reached the heart of the city. Everywhere fountains gush forth; at intersections, marble groupings mime acts of Commerce, Industry, Banking. From theaters with vast cupolas come snatches of opulent hubbub, while from concert halls, the potbellied opera house, hymns rise to reach their ears.

Clusters of men and women bring these settings to life, as if there only in illustration. A couple exits a nightclub. Beneath the fringed canopy, between planters of painted wood, a man in a frock coat slips a doorman a fortune. At a wave, a horse and buggy parked nearby springs to life, pulling in by the sidewalk. The doorman hurries over. The lady folds the ends of her stole over her breast; her jewels sparkle, her ankle boots gleam in the gaslight. The gentleman climbs in behind her. The buggy rounds a bend in the avenue and disappears. Farther down, legislators out late from a meeting congratulate one another on the steps of a government edifice before going their separate ways, each scurrying off to their own waiting carriage. In the windows, lights still burn. Elsewhere, lovers stand entwined under arcades. Heads bow, hands clasp. A solitary walker, head bare, whistles a tune. On the fiacre's cushions, the man in black has remained silent till now. The youth has followed suit, intent on the spectacle of the streets.

"You've never been here before?"

"No, but it's the most beautiful city I've ever seen. At least this part is. The outskirts look like any other city, gray and ugly."

"You don't like cities."

"Yes! No … Oh, I don't know. I don't really care. City or country, it's all the same, so long as there's food to eat!"

"Don't worry, we'll feed you. Just a few minutes longer now."

The boy leans out the window. They've passed the city's artistic and administrative heart and now glide past dwellings, here and there dotting verdant estates in a residential borough.

"Well, here we are."

"Here? Do you really mean it?"

"Yes. What were you expecting?"

"Oh, nothing, nothing … This is your house?"

"No. But here I can do as I please."

The mansion is tall and vast, behind bronze gates. Marble columns buttress the roof where it overhangs the terrace. In the courtyard, scores of carriages stand in neat rows, several adorned with crowns and coats-of-arms on their doors. Valets in wigs and livery form a guard of honor the length of the staircase. Laughter, the sounds of voices, snatches of music wing their way from drawing rooms and ring afar in the night air. The youth looks down at his dirty shirt and frayed pants; he hides his hands.

"They'll never let me in . . ."

"Don't you worry about that. Look, I'm no better dressed than you are. None of that matters, you'll see."

They descend from the fiacre. The footmen look on as they climb the steps, the boy careful to stay close beside the man. In the foyer, an usher comes to meet them. The man takes the usher aside for a moment, whispering something in his ear that the boy can't hear. The usher bows.

"Sir, my masters will be proud and delighted to welcome you, and might I, too, in my humble fashion, share in their joy, if you would be so kind . . ."

The man thanks him with a slight nod. "This young man is my aide."

"Ah! This way, gentlemen, please! Follow me . . ."

They fall in step behind him. At the entrance to the grand salon, the porter comes to a halt and announces them in firm, serious tones.

"The honorable messenger, accompanied by his honorable aide!"

At once, the bustle of conversation falls silent. The pianist stops playing and shuts the fallboard. Everywhere, glasses of wine and hands of cards are set down; eyes turn toward them. A murmur of respect runs through those assembled. Man and boy make their way beneath the chandeliers. The youth does his best not to slip on the gleaming parquet. The man, for his part, seems entirely at ease, and the youth envies him his sureness of step, his nonchalance of bearing. His haversack slaps his threadbare cloak, and a cocksure little smile hovers on his lips. The mistress of the house, aflutter as if at a visiting prince—which may well be the case, the young drifter thinks—hurries to greet them. The man bows, but not as deeply as she curtsies. The inexplicable deference everyone has shown them since their entrance goes to the boy's head. And here she is, this grand dame, insisting on curtsying before him, and showering him—him too!—with countless courtesies. He stammers some nonsense in return, she is happy, flattered; he lets himself be congratulated, they are dragging him toward the buffet.

"You must be starving to death! Oh yes, yes, right this way, we'll take care of you. Ladies, if you please!" The mistress of the house claps her hands. "Ladies, ladies! Come now, where are your heads? We must keep this young man company. He is the honorable messenger's right hand! Come, come, one and all, have no fear! Don't be afraid. He's a big boy, but he won't bite."

Adorable young women flock about him. He is shown to a seat. A young lady on his right ensures his flute always brims with champagne. Two others on his left, dressed in mauve and lemon yellow, hand him plates of tiny sandwiches, pâté en croute, and petits fours. Ten more, every shade of the rainbow, bustle about before and behind, laughingly vying for the privilege of bringing him a napkin, a knife, a silver teaspoon. Utterly bedazzled, he grandstands, jests between mouthfuls, drinks from his bottomless flute, sampling every delicious tidbit served up to him. Meanwhile, the messenger receives tribute from the gathered society, every last person insisting on a word. Women blush, breathing harder in their corsets when their turn comes to approach the great man. The men, more somber, straighten up, set their jaws, do their best to adopt a vaguely martial air, as if to commune in his company with some heroic ambiance. Steadily gorging himself and holding forth before his court of admirers, the boy casts about for the man now and then, abruptly flooded with fear he might vanish, and with him this delectable aura of glory. But the man is still there, not far away, still feted, still in demand, now and then giving him a furtive wink, ironic yet benevolent all at once, as if to say: Well, what do you think? See how they love us? Enjoy it all, stuff yourself with tasty things, get smashed on champagne and those sweethearts' darling smiles, boast and bluster, have fun!

And the boy smiles back, mouth full, head spinning from the lights, the laughter, the carousel of coquettes. At last, the man reaches the end of his civilities.

"Friends! My friends! Please, we must give the honorable messenger a chance to breathe! That's right, here we are, pressing up to him, hemming him in, without a thought for the weariness of a world traveler. Please, I beg of you, give him space. He has promised to stay, he shall be our guest all night. Let us be sparing with him!"

At these injunctions from the lady of the house, the crowd regretfully scatters. Conversations resume at a slight distance, animated, all centering on this unexpected visit. If only they'd known! But how could they have? And isn't that always the way? No matter where he goes, he never gives notice. Naturally, the demands of his mission, the secrecy of his movements, naturally . . . Someone goes to fetch the musicians. They gather on the stage beside the pianist. Gallantly, the messenger offers his hostess his arm.

"Oh, dear friend, I'm simply dying to! But do you really wish to dance, after such a long journey? You must be exhausted!"

"Not at all, not at all! I insist on opening this ball with you. Will you grant me the pleasure?"

Couples have already formed on either side of the floor. The musicians signal their readiness. The lady of the house soars on the messenger's arm, beaming with pride as her friends look enviously on. One by one, other couples join in, breaking away from the colorful bed of onlookers like bouquets tossed on a whim into the music's whirlwind. His hunger more or less appeased, the youth contemplates, as he drains his flute, the circlings of the messenger and his partner. The man dances rather poorly, but couldn't care less, and the boy credulously admires the man who opened wide the doors to such a world for him. No one, for that matter, seems to notice how clumsy a dancer the man is, nor how ridiculous a sight the haversack still on him makes as it flaps and smacks against his side every time the couple whirls in their waltz.

"And you, sir, do you like to dance? Waltzes are so very beautiful!"

The damsel in mauve awaits his answer. To be sure, the honorable aide's opinion on the waltz, as on all things in general, is of the utmost importance to her tonight. But he does not know how to dance. He takes one last swig of champagne, clears his throat, and in a shaky voice replies, "Oh, I quite agree, Miss, it's very pretty to watch. Truly enchanting!"

The damsel in mauve smiles with pleasure. But she always smiles, no matter what he says. Perhaps she smiles like that all the time, from morning till night, even alone, and deep into her dreams at night. He prefers, however, to credit himself for that radiant face. She is wild about him, he fancies, there's the truth of it; the mere fact of his presence transfigures her so. Otherwise, she is secretive and shy, even given to melancholy. She probably loves poetry, aviaries, tears, and he, oafish boy that he is, accustomed only to the hardships of the road, feels altogether ready to love such things too if only to please her. She leans on the armrest of his chair, bending closer toward him, without a care for the daggers her companions stare. The scent of violets wafts from a Parma bouquet pinned to her hair.

"You must be a wonderful dancer."

The boy's face clouds over. He doesn't dare lie. "Er . . . truth to tell, no, not really. I hardly have time to practice, you know."

"Oh, of course, I understand. Your mission!"

"Precisely! My mission. Our mission, I mean . . ."

The young lady nods earnestly. Her smile fades at once, giving way to a serious expression as might befit the thought of such terrible things. But the boy likes her better when she smiles. He waves his hand as if to dispel her cloud of worries.

"Let us speak of it no more. I'll soon have time enough to think on it, and besides, it's a secret . . . You see what I'm getting to at? Don't take it the wrong way."

"Not at all! Why, I would never! Forgive me, you mustn't think I'm being nosy. All this is far too serious. Please know I respect your silence, of that you can be sure! Instead, let us speak of—dancing! So you don't get to dance much? How dreadful for you! Why, I couldn't go a day without dancing. I have dance class every morning—dancing is my whole life! Ah, dancing, dancing!" Upon uttering these last few words with grandiloquent fervor, she shuts her eyes and swoons. The other girls around her have had enough. Seizing her chance to turn his head, the lemon-yellow damsel gives a shrug.

"Poor dear, why you're boring him silly, nattering on about dancing! I'm sure he much prefers horseback riding. The honorable aide must be a wonderful rider, isn't that so? Why, it's obvious. Oh, yes, you can tell such things, when you've spent a little time in the saddle yourself. This very morning I mounted a splendid beast at the riding hall. Truly splendid! You should have seen him . . ."

The damsel in mauve digs her heels in deeper, as she finds the attack well-timed and fears the young man's attention will shift from her to the equestrienne.

"Oh, what would you know? He sees horses all the livelong day. They must grow so dreadfully boring. Ah, but dancing! Dance with me, good sir, won't you please? Oh, please? They say I dance the waltz very well, and that's what they're playing."

"But—"

"Oh, please?"

Already she leads him toward the floor. Awkwardly, he takes hold of her waist. She laughs.

"No, not like that! Here, give me your hand. I'll lead at first, if you like, till you find your footing. There, now we may begin. Let me guide you. Relax."

The youth follows her as best he can, but his feet are not so quick to shake off the hobo in hobnailed boots.

Time and again he sees her suppress a grimace of pain and deduces that he's stepped on her feet in their lacquered heels. Still, the young woman perseveres, darting victorious glances at her companions.

"Good, very good. You catch on quick."

"Oh, no, I'm well aware I keep stepping on your feet. I'm just too clumsy. Why don't we go for a stroll on the grounds instead?"

But the damsel in mauve, wishing to flaunt her victory over the equestrienne, begs for at least one valedictory lap around the floor. He complies. Now and then their lumbering movements—for truly, he has two left feet—bring them close to the messenger who, still saddled with his haversack, sends the evening's loveliest ladies twirling about, one after the next. The man dances with his eyes half-closed, tightly clasping his partner of the moment. But from a corner of the room, another man signals him discreetly. The messenger sees. With the slightest tilt of his chin, he indicates his partner; he can't just leave her there. Other couples come between them and the boy, concealing them from view.

"There. That wasn't so hard, was it? You acquitted yourself quite well."

The mauve damsel is still smiling, but rather less from pleasure than relief, he suspects. They have finished the final lap they'd embarked on, and their voluntary torture—embarrassment for him and discomfort for her—is at an end. They leave the dance floor. Nearby, the messenger's partner is refreshing herself with a sorbet. The messenger himself has slipped away, probably with the other man who signaled to him earlier. All of a sudden, the youth feels lost among these too-elegant strangers. The filth on the rags he wears, forgotten in the warmth of their welcome, comes back to mind, along with his gaucherie, his ignorance of good manners. Here he is, understanding next to nothing, but nothing—and what if someone were to inquire about his so-called mission, or some other serious subject of widespread interest? Luckily, the mauve damsel draws him into a vestibule off to one side.

"Come, sir! No doubt you're unfamiliar with the house? Allow me to give you a tour, if you'd like."

"Yes, gladly, but please don't go to any trouble. Maybe you'd rather be with your friends, or do some more dancing . . . with a different partner, I mean!"

"No, no, forget my friends. I know those ninnies all too well. As for dancing, I confess I don't quite feel up to it tonight. Besides, it would be an honor to show you around the premises."

"You seem to know them well. Do you come here often? Whose house is this, anyway?"

For a moment, the girl seems surprised. Her brow creases in bafflement and displeasure. The youth hastens to apologize for his faux pas.

"It's just that the messenger, my master, never tells me anything in advance, and since we arrived late, as you know, in all the hubbub . . . He keeps secrets, even from me, though I go where he goes, like a shadow!"

"Yes, yes, I see. Well, this is my house—my father's, that is. The alderman . . ."

She eyes him, watching his face for a reaction, which he surmises should be one of awe and admiration, lest he offend her. He conforms to these expectations, though never before has he heard of this august personage. His eyebrows shoot up and he tilts his head to one side, as if the better to admire her in the radiance this revelation affords.

"Oh, my! Well, then! The alderman! Which would make you his daughter! How proud you must be!"

"My word! A little, I'll confess. There are but three aldermen in the entire realm, and my father is the second most influential. The papers say he'll rise even higher in the ranks, very high indeed, just how high who can say . . ."

"Tell me more! Why, here comes your friend, the lady in lemon. Shall I call her over? No doubt she'll want to come with us."

"No, don't call her, she'll talk our ears off about riding . . . Or rather, do! Call her over, and let's hide. We'll give her the old runaround. It'll be such fun!"

The youth returns to the hall's entrance. "Yoohoo! Miss! Over here! We're waiting for you!"

The young woman, who has clearly been scanning the crowd, spots him and smiles. She scurries toward him.

"Here she comes! Quick, hurry!"

The mauve damsel pulls him by the sleeve into the depths of the vestibule. He hesitates. "This doesn't seem very nice . . ."

"And she is? She's nice? Oh that's right, you've never seen her true colors. She can be such a cow! Come on, she's going to catch up!"

He lets himself be led toward a stone staircase that seems to sink straight into the earth.

"Down there?"

"Yes, down here. These are the cellars. They're huge, you'll see. They cover an area greater than even the house itself. You could get lost there if you don't know your way around. Wait!"

Hastily, the girl climbs back up the few steps they've just gone down, takes the tiny bouquet of violets from her hair, plucks one out, and places it in an obvious spot on the landing before descending once more.

"Otherwise, she won't think to follow us down here. Now let's hurry. I can hear her coming."

The steps are steep and narrow. The masonry returns their footfalls in endless echo. Never before has the youth seen such foundations. At every landing, candle stubs cast a feeble glow on the first steps of each new flight, and then, in the gloom, he must trust a banister coming away in brown flakes beneath his hand. He soon loses count of the landings. The deeper they go into the bowels of the house, the colder it grows; he shivers in his rags. He would like to go back up. Even if she's spotted the flower they'd left her in acknowledgment, the young lady in yellow will doubtless have given up, put off by the unending descent, the cold, the isolation. Despite his protests, the girl in mauve leads him ever lower. Her dress, earlier so fresh and becoming beneath the main hall's chandeliers, has turned in the low light, taking on a vinous tinge that pales her too-fair skin to chalk.

"No, I just know she's following us! Come on! Are you scared of rats, like a little boy? They're almost all gone now, hunted down on my father's orders. And a merciless hunt it was: traps, cats, and poison. Poor rats! I for one never hated them. They'd scamper about quietly, keeping to themselves; I'd bring them lard in secret. They'd come to me, twitch the tips of their little noses, but they never stayed around for long. Off they'd run again, to savor the lard at their leisure in their holes. As for the cats . . . that's a different story, you'll see. It's crawling with cats down there—caterwauling, calling out to each other. I don't like them. Ah, here we are."

At the foot of the stairs, a crypt of colossal breadth and depth, low-ceilinged to a fault, stretches before them. Before, behind, on every side, lines of columns divide it into narrow gravel-strewn aisles that alternate with rows of cages chained fast to four columns and suspended beneath the vault they bear. Guttering candle-ends like those on the stairwell, alcoved halfway up the columns here and there, shed a faint light on the cages. The aisles, lost to darkness in the distance, might go on forever, as the obsessive regularity of the layout leads one to believe. Everywhere, cats haunt the aisles, as promised, prowling or dozing in gangs of three or four. Now and again, some fight over a female.

"Big, isn't it? Even I've never been all the way to the end. Though I've come here often, ever since earliest childhood. I keep pushing on and on past the cages, and then, at some point, I get scared; I can't help it. Scared I won't be able to get back, scared I'll lose my way and have to keep wandering among the cages like this for the rest of my life. Silly, I know, there must be at least one other exit somewhere, but I can't help it, I get scared. There are plenty of people down here, you know."

"Oh, really? Prisoners?"

"Prisoners, lodgers, I don't really know, they never answer your questions, or else they jabber nonsense. But most are mute. My father's men bring them food once a week. It's also a chance to clean out their cages, and well, that's all there is to it. Do you find them interesting? Forget it, they won't say a thing. They never complain. You'd think they're happy down here like this, after all. Come along, you'll have plenty of time to stare. But whatever you do, don't forget to mark the way we came!"

From the little bouquet she's kept in hand ever since the vestibule, she plucks a second flower and sets it on the gravel at the head of an aisle.

"Now, quickly! Let's switch aisles!"

They run, scattering in their wake many a coterie of tubby angoras who melt away into the shadows.

"She'll be here any minute!"

"She should be here already! She must have given up, if you ask me. Does she know this place?"

"Yes, I've brought her down many a time. We'd come feed the rats or have fun maddening the lodgers. On her own, she's a scaredy-cat, but she wants to be with us too badly to turn back. Look, there she is!"

The lemon-yellow damsel appears at the foot of the stairs. Together, boy and girl duck around the corner of the first cage and spy on her through the bars. The young woman takes a few steps toward the cages. The color of her dress has altered now, too, in the pallor. She stops, disappointed. She was expecting to find them straightaway. She grows worried. Her voice rises, thin and reedy, beneath the oppressive vaults.

"Hello! Hellooo! Where are you two?"

For a moment she waits, and then, since no voice answers, she boldly steps forward. She spots the violet, picks it up, then brings it to her face to breathe in the aroma—nonchalantly, she hopes, for she can sense them nearby, watching her, and wants to make the right impression.

"Yoo-hoo! Where are you? Is this a game?"

"Maybe!"

The young woman gives a start. After calling out, the mauve damsel beats a swift retreat, the boy in tow. The lemon damsel's voice reaches them once more, less distinctly through the distance now between them.

"Sir? Please, won't you at least say something? Where are you? Is this a game?"

The youth cups his hands around his mouth. "Who knows?"

His companion grabs his wrist, giving it a tight squeeze of approval. Lips parted, too attentive, too avid for a mere game of hide-and-go-seek, the girl in mauve pricks up her ears for any calls from her lonesome friend; her eyes glitter. From the depths of the cage they crouch behind, a shape suddenly rears up. A weary sigh lightly ruffles their hair. The youth starts, the girl cannot suppress a cry of fear. Between two scurfy hands clutching the bars, a face wild with sorrow peers out at them. The mauve damsel stands up. Her lips twist in anger. She drives a stiff-fingered hand between the bars. With a grunt of pain, the pitiful specter retreats into the shadows. The young lady pulls her hand back. A bit of blood pearls on the sharp little blade of each fingernail.

"That brute! He scared me. Now she'll know where we are! Brute! Brute! Filthy swine! I'll make him pay!"

From a shapeless black mass huddled at the far corner of the cage come long sobs that only intensify each time the girl, in her rage, rattles the bars with a vicious kick. The sound of hurried footsteps rings out on the gravel of the neighboring aisle.

“Settle down! The girl in yellow’s heard everything. She’s close now, listen! She’s going to find us!”

“You’re right, let’s go. As for you—just you wait! I’m not through with you yet, do you hear? Filthy swine!”

The man whimpers in the darkness of his cage. The footsteps draw closer. Just as the lemon damsel is about to find them, boy and girl dash off down the narrow passageway leading to the next aisle. Gravel shrieks and surges from beneath their feet. The sounds of running speed up behind them, but the girl in mauve has already regained her composure.

“I know a way to lose her again. Let’s keep running for a bit, then come to a sudden stop. It works every time—you’ll see.”

This simple plan works like a charm. Their pursuer freezes in turn, disoriented by the unexpected silence. From where they hide, they can clearly hear her ragged breathing. She takes a few more steps, utterly lost now in the labyrinth of aisles and cages. She calls out to them. Her voice trembles with fatigue and doubtless, mounting anxiety as well.

“Yoo-hoo, you two! I know you’re out there! Let’s stop this game, I’ve had enough. I’m out of breath. Come out, come out, wherever you are! This isn’t very nice!”

The youth, tired too, and privately troubled by the mauve damsel’s immoderate passion for this diversion, pleads in whispers on the other girl’s behalf. But his partner will have none of it.

"Oh, no, not yet! We're having so much fun! Wait, I just had an idea."

Here and there, inside the cages all around them, shadows stir noiselessly. Doleful faces, brows pressed to the bars, gaze out at them. From time to time, the mauve damsel shakes her fist at them in annoyance. That is enough to discourage these timid watchers, who ebb fearfully back. Cats, too, living in peace with the lodgers, take refuge between legs or atop shoulders at the slightest gesture even a bit too abrupt from the intruders, on whom they turn green, unblinking eyes. Most of the cages are untenanted, but few indeed are completely bare. Many are piled with odds and ends: utensils, furniture, carafes and demijohns, boxes and crates, all empty or full, chipped or whole, hard to say: priceless antiques are jumbled together with junk. The only cages with closed doors contain a man inside. There are locks and padlocks of all shapes and sizes, deadbolts, locksets, spring locks, warded locks, heavy combination padlocks or cheap novelty locks smaller than the links in the chains where they dangle. With a quick glance, the mauve damsel selects a suitable cage, cluttered with a heap of crates drowned in darkness.

"Just what we need."

"We're going in there?"

"No, not us—*her*!"

The key is in the padlock. The young woman checks that it works. The youth looks on, not understanding what she has in mind. Why would the girl in lemon yellow climb inside that cage?

"But how . . . ?"

"She'll think we're in there, of course!"

She leaves the door ajar and, backing up a few steps on the gravel, lays her bait, the second-to-last of her violets. She steps away to take in her surroundings and gauge the efficacy of her trap. She seems satisfied. She takes the key from the padlock and clutches it tight in her fist. All is ready.

"Yoo-hoo! Yoo-hoo! Over here!"

With a swift shove, she sends the cage door flying at its iron frame and then, in the din of rattling bars, drags the boy to the nearest passageway. There, they flatten themselves on the ground, noses in the gravel, winded.

"There she is! Not a sound!"

At the ruckus, the lemon damsel comes running. For a moment, she wavers between the darkness of the passageway where the other two are hiding and the cage still quivering from the impact. But the violet catches her eye. She turns from the passageway to the aisle and plants herself squarely in front of the cage, hands on her hips. This time she doesn't bother picking up the flower, instead crushing it with her heel. The gravel's sharp edges shred the petals.

"Are you in there? I just know you're in there, behind those crates. Come out, come out, stop this stupid game! After all, we're not children anymore."

She studies the darkness inside the cage at length. All around her, lodgers and cats who have shrunk into the shadows, terrified by the mauve damsel's sudden movements, appear once more at the bars of their cages. The lemon damsel walks closer to the cage. Her fingers toy briefly with the padlock. A notion, a hope must have stirred, only to be snuffed at once, a vague, crafty yearning that never made it past the first impediment to fulfillment.

"You deserve to be locked away in there, do you hear? Lucky for you there's no key! But I've had enough. I'll come looking for you in your hole, since you won't come out yourselves."

She opens the door and steps into the cage. As she walks deeper into the trap, the boy feels the mauve damsel quivering with jubilation beside him. Deep in the cage, all is still in the mound of crates. The lemon damsel loses her patience. With one kick, then another, she rattles the entire jumble, flushing out a cat. Tail bristling, fur on end, it spits and claws on its way out, vanishing in two bounds. The young woman brings her hand to her mouth and sucks at her scratch. Behind her, the mauve damsel seizes upon her distraction to dash forward. Gravel crunches, the door to the cage crashes shut. The lemon damsel lets out a brief cry and makes for the exit, but it's too late. The click of the padlock echoes coldly in the darkness. The boy joins them. Unsurprisingly, their prisoner has grabbed the bars with both hands. At first, they are all silent. The mauve damsel seems uncertain in her moment of triumph. So it is that, once the thrill of the chase has passed, the hunter may wonder what they were after, and gazing upon the slain creature in the grass, suddenly doubt this was it. The victim stares down her tormentors one by one. The boy looks away. This game, which bored him already, now frankly disgusts him. What cause had he to go and share in his companion's obscure resentments? The silence drags on, confining the two youths in their complicity despite themselves. Even if they now wished it—and he at least would like to cut and run—they can no longer open the door and give the girl back her freedom without losing face.

"The bird has been caught, the pretty canary is in her cage! Will she sing? Sing, little canary, sing for your supper of seeds!"

His voice rings hollow when he speaks, his mockery half-hearted despite his intentions. The mauve damsel joins in, making his gibes her own, investing them with a cruelty she no longer bothers to conceal with a jesting air.

"Oh, good idea! That's it, make her sing for us. Sing, pretty bird, and we might give you the key, if your song wins us over."

"Oh, no! Please, not that, you know I can't carry a tune. I'd never have the nerve in front of the honorable aide. If it's a dare you want, pick something else, and then let me out. It's late. My parents upstairs will be worried."

The mauve damsel struts about in front of the cage, pretending to think it over, frowning, pulling faces. She has recovered all her verve, her haughtiness, ever since the boy quite inadvertently gave her the means to revel in her victory over her rival.

"Why, my pet, what makes you so sure this is a game? Honorable aide, good sir, are we playing a game?"

Once again, the boy plays along with the wink she gives him. "A game? My word, I can't be sure . . . Perhaps it is, after all. Perhaps it is!"

"Indeed! Nothing could be less certain. But let's have no more talk of that. You're going to have to sing, no matter what. Come now, don't be silly, show the 'honorable aide' how well you can sing. The gentleman promises to be lenient. Besides, think of the key! Think of your parents who must be getting worried indeed . . . Sing! We're listening!"

The lemon damsel wrings her hands. Cheeks bright red, gaze downcast, she gives in. "All right. But promise you'll—"

"Sing! We shall see."

"*The king had his drummers beat their drums*
The king had his drummers beat their drums
To see all his kingdom's la-a-adies . . .
And the first one he saw . . ."

"Stop! You started out too low! And you're out of tune! Put some effort into it, won't you? Once more, from the top! Try harder!"

The girl obeyed. "*The king had his drummers . . .*"

Her voice falters. His heart in his throat, the youth listens to that shrill, off-key voice struggle with each word, each note, before breaking off in a sob. He wants to do something.

"Enough!"

"Oh yes, right you are! She's no good at all, is she? She's making our ears bleed. Let's change up the drill. She'll chirp for us, like a little birdie. She'll chirp and chitter and twitter for us, and we'll have a good laugh! Go on! We're waiting, little bird! Remember—the key!"

"Tweet, tweet, tweet! Twitter tweet! Chirrup, chirrup cheep! Chirrupirrupeepeepeep! Cuckoo! Yoodle-ay-ee-oo! Tweet! Toodle-ay-ay-eep-eep-oo!"

The lemon damsel puffs out her cheeks and strains her voice in dubious mimicry made halting by sniffles and hiccups. Then, herself overcome by laughter as her tormentors' mirth grows, she redoubles her efforts, trying harder to satisfy them, desperate now, veering from tears to the fearful gaiety of a half-willing participant in her own humiliation. The mauve damsel could not be more overjoyed. She hops up and down, clinging to the bars, conveying her own excitement to her victim.

"Yes, yes, very good! Excellent! More, more, faster, higher—now cluck like a hen! No, meow, that's right, meow, very good! Why, she's wonderful! Now bark, yes, bark! Growl! Louder!"

"Meow! Meeeoooow! Meeeow! Woof! Woof woof arf! Grrrrrr! Grrrrrrr! Woof grrrr!"

"She's tremendous! Keep it up! Keep it up! Here's a flower, take it, eat it! Go on, eat it all up! Good dog!"

The lemon damsel snaps up the violet, crumpled and damp with sweat from the outstretched palm, as a dog might a scrap of meat.

"Enough! Enough! Stop it! You're out of your minds, both of you!"

With all his might, the boy slaps the mauve damsel across the face. She stumbles back a few steps, choking, incredulous, then stops in her tracks. Their victim, too, stands frozen behind bars, the stem of a violet still hanging from her lips. Her undone face, smudged with tears, betrays only stupefaction, and against this backdrop of disarray, for a fleeting second, an absurd annoyance shines through. *After all, she had the spotlight.* The alderman's daughter regains her wits. With a burst of pride, she has tamed her trembling lower lip and bitten back the tears springing to her eyes. No trace now remains of the respect she showed the youth not long before. She is but disdain and a thirst for vengeance.

"Forgive me, Miss, I didn't mean to. But it's also true we were going too far, that young woman doesn't deserve this. Why torment her so? The game's over. Give me the key, let's let her out. I—I hope I didn't hurt you too badly? I was only trying to calm you down. I'm sorry—"

"Yes, you hurt me! Badly! You're just a grubby little brute, I should've known! You hit me! Me, the alderman's daughter! At his house, in his home, when he was so kind as to take you in, you vagrant louse! You can bet you'll be sorry, believe me! Oh, yes, you'll be sorry, I'll make sure of that. And she'll be sorry too, both of you! Both of you, do you hear?"

The captive, hearing herself lumped in with the boy in the same threat, protests her good intentions. "But what did I do? I didn't do anything! I did as you said, I chirped, I barked, I ate the flower just like you wanted. We had good fun, didn't we? It was a game, all this was just a game between us, you and me, good friends, the tricks and pranks you played on me, you're such a tease! He's the stranger here, the lout you ought to punish. Just let me out of here and we'll play some more, I'll do anything you want, I'll help you get revenge on that buffoon, we'll go see your father together, I'll back up your story!"

"Do you think I need you? Poor little fool! Watch this!"

The mauve damsel raises a fist, still wrapped around the key, above her head. "Here!"

Her arm bends back, abruptly straightens. The key spins through the air beneath the vault. A distant clink of metal on metal. It must have fallen five or six aisles away, between the bars of a cage in the gloom. The lemon damsel weeps in silence, her brow pressed to the doorframe. The mauve damsel's eyes shine with sated hatred.

"There. And as for you, 'honorable aide,' you'll get yours. I bet my father will save one of these cages for you when he finds out you hit me. Unless he has his servants beat you to death, if I add that you slid your hands up my dress while whispering dirty words!"

With a single bound, she leaps from view into the next aisle over. The sound of her steps on the gravel bed soon grow faint. Silence falls. The boy hasn't even tried to give chase. He stands there, dumbfounded, arms dangling. Across from him, the lemon damsel gently sniffles and whimpers.

"This is all your fault. If only you hadn't slapped her, she might have had her fun a little while longer, then let me out. Why did you do that? Now it's over, the key is gone, I'll never get out of here ever again. Never again, do you hear?"

"Why—that's absurd!"

"That's how it is! My parents won't dare complain, the alderman's too powerful, my father would fear for his own position. He won't even know where I am, no one will ever know. It's over . . . over!"

"Don't be stupid. I'll look for the key. I'll find it. Besides, even if I can't, I'll go ask someone for help, a caretaker, a locksmith . . . We'll come get you out, I promise!"

"No. No one ever gets out. Oh, woe is me! How often I played here, among the cages, and now my turn has come . . ."

"But they have no right to keep you locked up here. You didn't do anything wrong!"

"What would you know about it? What would I know, myself? And the others, the others all around us, what did they ever do wrong? They don't know, no one does. Here they are, just like me, forever, and that's all there is to it. Go on, ask them why they're here! They can't remember anymore, if they ever knew to begin with. I'm already starting to doubt there was ever a sunlit world up there with meadows, rivers, trees . . . My God, my entire life has only ever been leading up to this cage! And where is yours leading you? Here, too, no doubt! Look around you, honorable aide, look, stare hard at these cages, study the bars, the locks, take a deep breath, flare your nostrils wide—don't you recognize that smell? No? Well, you soon will. Take a breath, look around, jog your memory! That face at the bars—doesn't it ring a bell? Isn't he your cellmate, haven't you seen him a thousand times before, furrowing his brow or scratching the tip of his nose? Here, feel this bar, this spot of rust right under your fingertips. You've spent days, weeks, months, years, scratching at it with your nail, making it bigger, making it look first like a heart and then a woman's privates, then a dog's head, then nothing, a circle, a circle you applied yourself endlessly to perfecting, enlarging, evening out the edges, and often the tiniest of glints would leap at your eye, disfiguring the work you'd almost finished, and you would start again, over and over, scratching with your nail, trimming away minuscule strips of rust! Oh, honorable aide! Have you found your cage yet? It's nice and quiet there, that's where we can safely rest, far from life and its chaos . . . For heaven's sake, what are you doing out there, in the middle of the aisle, outside your cage? Beware! Climb in, shut the door, throw the key down a distant aisle. Hurry!"

The lemon damsel falls to her knees before the locked door. The boy strokes her hair through the bars. She pushes his hand away.

"Be kind. Leave me."

The youth stands up. Visually, the crypt discourages any attempt he makes to orient himself. He no longer knows which way they came, and it matters little: there is no way he can retrace his steps. Manservants in wigs and powdered truncheons surely await him beneath the rotunda. No, he has but one chance at escaping this place, and that is finding another exit. He has lost all notion of time. Perhaps the festivities have come to an end upstairs, perhaps the sun has already risen over the city. The messenger will have left without him already, without even worrying about his absence. In truth, the man had never promised to take him into his service. And so even should the youth manage to get himself out of this predicament, everything will go back to the way it was before. He runs among the columns. Everywhere, the same proportion of empty cages to full seems to remain roughly constant: one for every four or five. And all around, the same pale faces rise up, the same mournful eyes blink as he goes by, countless cats vanish. He forces himself to run faster, heart pounding; gravel flies from beneath his hobnailed boots and rings against the columns, the bars. His vision blurs; in the aisle ahead, perspective loses its immutable integrity, starting to buckle and warp. With every step, the argands on the columns seem at times to cast off dazzling rays and at others to dwindle in blue sparks. Then everything goes dark. He manages a few yards blindly, arms outstretched, before his legs give out. He sinks into unconsciousness. When he recovers his wits, the corridor around him has returned to its usual appearance. He rises to his feet. Sixty feet away, the aisle comes to an end. He makes out a stairway like the one he had come down. Beyond stretch more aisles lined with more rows of cages. For a moment, he worries about a potential ambush, but all is quiet. He heads up, wasting no time in starting the long climb to fresh air. The landings keep coming. They look so much like the ones the mauve damsel dragged him down—same layout, same lighting, even the same texture to the masonry—that he begins to doubt he's found a different way out, half-expecting to emerge into the same vestibule. But at the top, he doesn't recognize the door. This one is narrower and upholstered in thick flowery fabric, while on the other, wood grain had shown through the varnish. He pricks up his ears, but the padding keeps him from hearing a thing. At his push, the door gives way in silence. The boy hazards a glance. Beneath the doused chandeliers, the room is deserted. At its far end, a lone figure stands out in the glow from a single torch. He is bent over a table, the only item of furniture not under a slipcover. Even at this distance, the youth spies the gray locks peeking out from beneath the man's hat. He starts toward him. His heavy boots ring out on the parquet. Halfway across the floor, he clears his throat.

"Sir . . . Master . . ."

The messenger says nothing. Has he even heard? The hall is vast. The boy falls silent. Just a few yards from the man now, he notices a folded blueprint in his hands. Beside him on the table, the haversack stands open. To the left, within reach, is a silver platter laden with glasses and a chilled bottle of champagne.

"Sir . . ."

"Yes, have a glass, help yourself." The messenger unfolds the blueprint. The boy does as he is told. The champagne runs lusciously down his throat, still raw from exertion. But no sooner does he drain his glass than the youth looks down in shame at the memory of his recent escapade.

"I have to tell you—"

"No, you don't. It's all the same to me."

"They must be out looking for me now, to give me a thrashing! But I didn't do anything wrong, the girl in mauve was lying, I swear!"

The messenger waves his hand to show how little he cares. "It matters little if she lied or not. Since you managed to escape the cellars, have no fear. In a few hours we'll be far away, and this house will be but a heap of ashes."

The youth stares at the man, dumbfounded. "What?"

"It's all going to burn. But drink some more champagne. We have time."

"But how . . . ?"

"You'll help me. We'll set fire everywhere, on every floor. Refill my glass, would you? I feel weary tonight. I'm going to need you."

The man rises. He steps back from the table and sweeps the room with his gaze: the walls adorned with paintings, the high ceilings where plaster putti flutter among acanthus leaves and cobwebbed fruit.

"Everything here must burn. It's not essential that you understand, of course. But tonight, I find myself overcome by a strange desire to speak. Like as not, I'm getting old. I am the messenger! You heard our hosts say so. See here . . . I've been on a mission forever, or almost. When I was entrusted with the message, I was about as old as you are now. I still don't know why I was chosen; a thousand others might've done just as well. I was no stronger or smarter than anyone else my age. Perhaps whatever fearsome power decreed the mission thought to discern in me more hidden gifts? Or else made do with the first fellow to come along? I know not. It matters not! In the beginning, I thought I would soon acquit myself of my task. It was all a game, I was heady with the secrecy, the heroism! There were coaching inns, contacts, passwords. Then from missed assignations to postponements, detours, countermands . . . time went by.

I was informed—oh, by means most mysterious!—that there was nothing pressing about the message despite its gravity; the crucial thing was that it reached its recipient *someday*. Does that sound absurd to you? I have wasted my life on this blind quest. Now and again, for months, years at a time, all traces would vanish. The man I was to meet could not be found, or had died, or gone mad, or else I would come to realize the town where we were to meet had never existed, or I would find nothing at the site but charred roofbeams, my contact's abode having burned to the ground the night before with all its lodgers. At such times I would retire for a while, never knowing if this hiatus in activity would prove definitive or if some morning another clue would return me to the road. I even started a family once, long ago. Then a man came to see me, and it was back in the saddle. But here—let's have another drink!"

"And now?"

"Patience. As I raced round the world on my errand—for my mission cares not a whit for borders or governments—I have been by arbitrary turns a pariah or, as here, a prince. I've been tossed in jail to rot, yanked out to be paraded triumphantly about on people's shoulders, and never with any clear idea of why. I've fought in wars, plotted this and that, fomented uprisings, planned surprise attacks, just to come across a horse thief or an imprisoned rioter who could set me back on my quest with a word. If I burn this mansion to the ground, it is because that is the price a political adversary of the alderman's has set for giving me information. That is the sole reason we are here."

"You mean to burn your host's house down for a mere bit of information?"

"Why not? My goal is to carry out my mission, not to protect the lives or holdings of anyone whatsoever."

"But accidents can always happen—"

"Will always happen, you mean! People will die. The alderman and his family have little chance of surviving the blaze; their bedrooms are on the fourth floor. Flames will be at their door before they've a chance to pull on dressing gowns. What of it? Will you plead for their lives? Don't bother; they will burn. But I have hope. I've traveled too many a road! There's no way I will die without meeting the message's intended recipient, and tonight, I am close to my goal; I can feel it. And you shall help me, by means fair or foul! In exchange for this crime, I shall obtain their address. I shall give them this sealed scroll that has been tossing about forever in the bottom of my haversack; they will take it, and I won't even bother trying to read over their shoulder. I'll be on my way, my soul at peace. But it is time. Look—we are here!"

With a finger, he points out the ballroom on the blueprint. The boy bends forward. Here, there, everywhere, scattered blindly about at first glance but upon closer inspection, the work of far more than mere whim, are marks the man has penciled in red wax on the layout of every level. From garret to ground floor, shrewdly sited and coordinated from one story to the next, they ring stairwells, bar doors, block hallways. The arsonist turns the inferno's score this way and that in his hands.

"Are you listening? We'll divvy up the work; I'll go up one side, you the other. Take half of the blueprint with you, just to be sure. We'll start the fire, working our way methodically down from the attic until we get back here. I've seen to everything; we'll go up empty-handed, there are demijohns of alcohol awaiting us up there. Here's yours, I've x-ed the spot. One mark, one fire. Make sure not to miss any along the way. It's easy, you'll see: a quick splash of alcohol, a match, and move on to the next. Don't dawdle; the minute we reach the front steps, the whole structure will be ablaze. Oh, right—here, take this."

The messenger draws two fat boxes of matches from his haversack. He proffers the first to the boy.

"And afterward?"

"Afterward, meet me by the oak tree near the gardener's house. Then, we'll see."

The man buckles his haversack, slings it across his chest. He tears the blueprint into two roughly equal parts, each with a route traced on it. He gives one to his companion.

Before leaving the room, the youth puts out the torch, an absurd gesture. In the darkened foyer, the messenger points to a set of double doors.

"Now go."

The messenger walks away. For a moment, his footsteps echo in the corridor. The boy pushes open one of the doors and hesitantly climbs the first few steps. Not that he's in any danger of falling; a single brass banister snakes from one landing to the next. No, it is something else, a singular leadenness to his limbs, a resistance the night itself pits against him like an immovable tempest. And yet he advances, one step at a time, bent and shivering, half-suffocating in the mealy murk, stopping only to strike a match and check the blueprint for the way to the attic. It lies beyond a door at the end of a hallway leading past the master bedrooms: a narrow stair flung without banisters toward the raftered heights. He climbs for a long time, every step risking a blind plunge into the dark. At long last, to his left, a glimmer takes shape, vague at first and then spreading as he mounts. The messenger, swifter, is already hard at it. The youth climbs the last few steps and emerges onto a vast platform. A peek at the plans confirms it as spanning the entire length and breadth of the house. Among the wooden pillars holding up the roof is a figure busily lighting fires. At the foot of the closest pillar, the youth recognizes two demijohns as the ones the messenger had mentioned earlier. He reaches for the first, meant for the attic alone. It is heavy.

He grabs it with both hands. Sweat starts beading on his forehead as he hops about, loosing brief spurts of alcohol onto the raw wooden floorboards. Flames the messenger has already sown light the attic bright as day. The youth hastens his step; the messenger warned him such seeds were quick to blossom. The heady alcohol fumes sting his nostrils. As he spatters the floor, the demijohn grows lighter in his arms, and the oppressive unease he felt on the climb fades. Soon he sets the demijohn, three-quarters empty, beside the first, still full, and retraces his steps among the pungent puddles splashed but yards apart from one another. He has chosen a spot deep in one corner of the attic for lighting the first match. From a distance, he tosses it into the puddle and shrinks back in fear at the first rush of flame. He shuts his eyes. When he opens them again, little blue and yellow blazes are already nipping at the floorboards. Quickly, he springs into action, striking matches as he moves, wasting three at a time on each puddle; soon thirty fires spring up in his wake. The heat rises; he dances among the flames, half blinded by smoke and sweat. Finally, he reaches the pillar. He seizes the full demijohn and drags it to the stairwell before going back for the second, whose contents he spills on the steps. Then he tosses it aside and, hoisting the first in his arms, starts down. Fifteen steps or so and he stops; still hugging the demijohn, he strikes a match and flicks it over one shoulder. But he has miscalculated the number of steps soaked in alcohol. A streak of flame tears down the stairs, singeing his pant cuffs, snapping at his calves on the way, snuffing out only a few yards lower. He totters. The demijohn almost slips his grasp. He hurries, feet in the flames, but upon reaching dry wood, these continue their progress down the stairs. He dares not run, for fear of waking the whole household with the pounding of his steps. Flames and arsonist reach the last step at the same time. Out of breath, the youth opens the door, steps over the sill, and shuts it behind him, finally setting down the demijohn to put out the flamelets at his ankles. No one has stirred. He can make out the breathing of peaceful slumber from behind each door. But at his back is the flames' dull roar. He starts moving again, leaving a spurt of alcohol at every doorsill. Then, carefully, he drenches the rug and baseboards till he reaches the landing. With the first match, a trickle of flame darts from door to door; then the entire hallway is ablaze. The youth picks up the demijohn he's safely stowed in the stairwell, a few steps from the landing. Time is short. He works backward, bent over, lighting fire after fire, pausing now and then to check the blueprint. He reaches the ground floor. Above him, all is conflagration. The first screams, the first stampedings resound from the upper stories. He locks the foyer door on those now doomed. The hallway the messenger headed down when they'd split up now vomits swirling black smoke. In the ballroom, yowling flames taunt the gala's couples, and floorboards splinter under the dancers' heels.

The cherubs on the walls blacken and crumble, the paintings take on uncanny hues before bursting into flames. The chandeliers collapse, their glassworks jangling. The messenger has been quicker and covered more ground. From the doorsill, the youth sends his demijohn spinning with a mighty heave into the middle of the room. It explodes. The spray of alcohol further fuels the fire. From a cornice cracked by heat a final cherub falls, its plaster wings parted. The youth hurls his box of matches and his balled-up half of the blueprint into the inferno. Then he crosses the foyer at a tear. From behind the door he's bolted shut come screams, thronging, something like trampling. Violent shoves rattle the double doors but fail to force them wide. He doesn't tarry. One leap and he's outside, on the steps. Men are running from neighboring dwellings. The fire, now ravaging the roof and topmost floors, casts shifting tarns of light on the lawn, fleeting puddles, streams that sometimes make the gravel paths their bed and then veer off at whims of wind and flame. The brass key is still in the front door lock. Doubtless the messenger has left him this one last task. The youth pushes the heavy door shut, turns the key twice, and pockets it. The first firefighters are now on the grounds. The youth rushes to meet them. They have buckets, ewers in hand; more arrive on their heels, bowed beneath a ladder's weight. A woman sweeps by in a nightgown, arms full of bandage rolls, cotton gauze, ointment.

"Quick, quick, hurry! I don't have anything, I'm going for help!"

They nod, not slowing. Under cover of their panic, the youth darts among the trees and into the night. From caution, he gives the gardener's house a wide berth; all its windows are lighted and several shadows moving off at a run toward the master's house. Set back a bit farther off stands the oak beneath whose leaves he makes out two figures, men seemingly untouched by the general alarm, content to witness the spectacle from a distance. He approaches them. One of them turns his head. A look of concern comes over his face, and he makes as if to flee, but the other stills him with a word. The youth joins them. The messenger acknowledges him with a nod while the other man, face masked, resumes his contemplation of the flames, not sparing the boy so much as a glance.

"Well done. Perfect! Oh, and before I forget—you made sure to block every last exit?"

The messenger turns to the boy, a question in his eyes.

"Yes. I locked the front door on my way out."

The stranger grunts with satisfaction. In silence, the three partners-in-crime behold the vain attempts at rescue. The people locked inside have no choice but to defenestrate themselves, and many burst from bay windows on the first and second stories, but those on higher floors, trapped in their rooms by flames, are hesitant to leap into the void. Sometimes one risks it all, hoisting up a nightgown. Several shattered bodies already litter the lawn.

Many must have perished from suffocation and burned in their sheets, for several windows remain shut, tongues of flame lapping at them from the inside. The survivors, wounded or too much in shock to reach the rescuers, have huddled in the middle of the lawn. A chorus of whimpering, sobs, wild words rises up toward heavens streaked with light. Beneath the oak, the messenger breaks the silence.

"Are you satisfied?"

Regretfully, the other man tears himself away from the spectacle of the conflagration and pulls the messenger to one side. They speak in low voices for a moment, then plunge swiftly into a thicket of trees with not a care for the boy, who falls in step behind. Nearby, beneath an arbor of ivy, two saddled horses await. At first the youth thinks one is his, as per the terms of his deal with the messenger. But the masked man betrays these expectations, setting foot in the stirrup. Behind them, a clamor of terror breaks out even as a long cracking sound is heard. The wind brings the smell of hot stone, charred wood and flesh. Without a word, the youth launches himself at the masked man. They fall to the ground, rolling between the horse's legs. The messenger does not intervene. First he leads his horse to one side, beside the arbor, to watch the struggle at his leisure. But soon, as neither rival seems able to bring things to a swift close, he spurs his mount, rounds the entangled combatants, and vanishes into the undergrowth. The masked man is hardy. His blows, from hand and foot alike, cruelly bruise the flagging youth's flesh. Blood runs from his nose and lips; a clout has shut one eye. His only thought now is for the fight to end; he begs the man to spare his life, but carried away by the heat of battle, his opponent is now bent on killing him. The horse has moved a few yards off and is grazing on the tender buds of hedges. Now and again, it turns its big, placid eyes toward the ballet of shadows. To finish things off, the man grabs a pronged hoe left lying in the grass. Once, twice, the youth dodges the terrible head with its iron tines. Icy sweat drenches his shirt; his jaw is clenched. The man gathers himself for a final assault. He rushes the boy, weapon held high. In three steps, he is upon him, but skids on the dew-slick grass. The hoe slips his grasp, he falls. Summoning all his strength, the youth kicks him in the head several times with his hobnailed boots. Something cracks from the blows. The man lies still. The youth approaches the horse, cajoling it in low tones, patting its neck. The creature docilely allows him to mount. The youth rides it down the path the messenger took, beneath the trees, toward the rear of the property, where a high wall capped with glass shards edges the grounds. He makes his way along the wall for a while before coming to an exit. An iron gate yawns wide on the linden-lined path that rings the demesne. The portal is too low for a mounted rider. He gets off the horse and leads it by the bridle down the deserted path. Across the way, similar walls guard other vast estates, their rooflines vaguely visible among the treetops. The youth climbs back in the saddle and urges the creature sharply forward through the silent night. On either side of the leafy lane, the residential borough's handsome dwellings soon grow fewer and farther between as his mount keeps up his insistent pace. He is now galloping past shorn fields, the sky slowly brightening on the horizon. Wind from his speed whips his face and plasters tangled curls to his brow. In the cool dawn, spouts of vapor shoot from his horse's nostrils; straight ahead, a red sun dispels the darkness. His heart beats harder, he is flooded with unreasoning joy at the sight of a figure beneath a tree, beside a horse whose silver coat gleams in the rising sun. At his approach, the man lifts the brim of his hat from his brow.

"Is that you, boy?"

"Yes. The man's dead, I think."

The messenger gives a nod. "I wouldn't have staked a farthing on you."

"Oh, he was much stronger, but he slipped and fell. So I killed him. You don't . . . hold it against me?"

"Why would I?"

"I don't know. Just because . . ." The youth waves his hand vaguely. The messenger rises to his feet. He saddles his horse, then slings his haversack over one shoulder and across his chest.

"I found out what I wanted to know. The rest is none of my concern."

"Did you really? He gave you the address? The real address?"

"Perhaps. I'll soon find out."

The youth canters about the man as he checks the tightness of the saddle strap.

"And is it . . . far from here?"

"No. Quite near."

"May I go with you? I could prove useful, you never know. And besides, I've got nothing better to do. I don't know where to go now."

The messenger turns toward him and studies him at length. Despite himself, the boy blushes under the fixed stare. The silence between them threatens to stretch on. One horse snorts, perhaps hastening the messenger's reply, or else altering it entirely. He puts one foot in the stirrup.

"I don't need anyone."

In the saddle now, he moves off at a light trot, unhurried, into a morn growing ever lighter by the moment. The youth takes to the road again in turn. A hundred feet ahead, the haversack bounces lightly at the small of the man's back, to the swaying of his hips. The land around them grows lusher: stands of trees, taller now and shaggier, multiply and merge as the last parcels of plowed earth, ceding their handsome rows to the woods' advance, succumb to bramble and stony debris. After a bit, the messenger leaves the road for a forest trail. The youth stills his horse at the entrance to the shadowed path, its vault of foliage pricked by pale rays of rising sun. There, in the umbrage, the messenger has stopped too, awaiting a decision, half-turned in the saddle and spying over one shoulder. At first, the boy hesitates; then, with a reckless kick, he spurs his mount among the trees. The messenger remains impassive. He waits till the youth has caught up, then urges his mount on with a slap. Silently, they make their way side by side through the shadows for a spell. Dead leaves carpet the soil on which the horses' hooves sometimes slide. Branches crack, creatures grunt in the underbrush, a hare bolts across the path. Straight ahead, the tunnel of greenery ends in a circle of light.

"We'll be there shortly. Have you ever heard tell of Le Grand B.?"

"Never. Is that where we—where you're going?"

"That is where we are headed. A curious spot indeed, it seems. Spoken of only in hushed tones. A house of pleasure, in theory, but one unlike any other. They say that once you've set foot inside, it's never certain you'll find your way out. About Le Grand B., rumors abound, all vague, all unsettling. Some, it is said, lost the faculty of sight there, others of speech, and others still of memory. Some were simply never seen again. Nor did anyone hurry to find them; the owner has friends in high places, it seems . . . Little matter! I am expected. By one unknown to me, but who shall make themselves known. We will stay as long as needed."

As they speak, the riders near the path's end. Briefly bedazzled, they ride down the final stretch of tunnel, aglow as if stoppered by light, and emerge into a vast basin-shaped clearing. Below, from a small isle in the middle of a lake, rises a manor whose walls and roof, smeared the same red ochre, are still steeped in shadow even as the sun's rays lap at the lake's edge. Strangely enough, the path comes to an abrupt halt at the meadow, as if human footsteps, horse's hooves, have never trod upon the grassy slope. The riders let the horses have their head, surrendering to the terrain's natural grade. The animals launch into a gallop, manes flying in the wind. The messenger gains a few lengths on the boy, but the slope is long, and the youth puts his utmost into closing the gap. Their eyes gleam, their cheeks flush at the air's sting. The messenger, too, joins in the sport. Blithely tearing a switch from a shrub, he whips his horse while urging it onward with shouts and spurs. But the youth speeds up in turn, and the distance between them dwindles. Soon they are neck and neck, letting out wild cries, cheering and haranguing their mounts. The horses charge onward, foaming at the mouth. The lake is near now. The sun, higher every moment, kindles the manor's ochre. Shutters are thrown wide and figures, hearkening to the incoming yawps, appear at unlatched casements. Just as the sun's rays light the tallest gable, the riders reach the shore. No bridge runs from solid ground to the isle. Still whooping with all their might, they turn sharply at the water's edge and begin to round the lake at full gallop. Every window has opened, one after the next, and now a throng of men and women behold their advance, leaning out over the railings. The messenger doffs his hat. Upright in his stirrups, he greets the company with breathtaking bows. His coattails flap in the wind, slapping his scrawny shanks; his gray hair flutters over his shoulders. Not to be outdone, the youth plays the clown, twirling and pirouetting atop his saddle at the risk of breaking his neck. From the house, they are answered with great friendly waves, ovations, a fluttering of handkerchiefs. Despite the early hour, the guests of Le Grand B. are fully dressed, the boarders in brocade, satin, velour of all colors, faces made up, hair done up as if for evening festivities. The women's tresses are flecked with as many flowers as the upholstered walls: bright buttercup yellow, soft rose gold, chestnut and ginger, auburn and strawberry blonde, every shade of brown through to black. And they are all cheering, blowing kisses. The men, many of whose faces are hidden behind scarves and domino masks, rhapsodize over the messenger's equestrian daring and gladly laugh at the boy's antics. Thus feted, man and youth make three rounds of the lake. At last, the messenger dismounts, and the boy follows suit. At that very moment, the women fall silent, their arms outstretched; the handkerchiefs waft to the ground. The worn-out horses wheeze like bellows. From the isle, a hundred pairs of eyes look on at the two unmoving figures by the water's edge. Then, in the silence, the clack of a shutter. In a matter of moments, every window in the ochre-red house is shut. The messenger sits down in the grass a few steps from the lake.

"What now?"

"We wait. Someone will come for us, I suppose. You ought to have a seat. This might take a while."

The youth takes the man's advice, even stretching out, and nods off, laid low at once by exhaustion from the ride after two nights in a row without sleep. Time passes. The boy snores, sometimes brushing a cricket or fly from his cheek without waking. The messenger chews a blade of grass, sitting cross-legged, facing the silent manor. For a long time, nothing stirs. The sun is at its zenith when a door creaks open beneath the veranda. A man comes down the front steps, turns left, and without so much as a glance at the messenger staring fixedly at him, vanishes around the side of the house. A few moments later, a stirring of water at regular intervals hints at a rowboat's approach. The messenger rouses his companion with a shove. The youth rubs his eyes.

"What's happening?"

At the sound of the oars, he understands and falls silent. Side by side, man and boy watch as the rowboat swings into view from around the isle. The man in the boat has his back to them, rowing at a leisurely pace. At first, all they can make out of him is his hunched back, topped by a round hat. Then, as he turns and pulls in the oars a few yards from shore to let the craft drift aground, they have plenty of time to note his brutish features beneath a thick thatch of unkempt hair. The prow sinks into the soft clay bank. The man hops onto dry land and holds out a sizable mitt in utter silence. From inside his jacket, the messenger pulls out a bulging purse and drops it into the outstretched palm. Without opening it, the man jingles it beside his ear and grins. Then he turns to the youth and holds out his other hand. The boy is taken aback. He has nothing! But at the messenger's gesture of encouragement, he nevertheless turns out his pockets. In one of them he finds a bronze penny, in the other a large key. He hands them over. The ferryman accepts them both, then stalks back down to the rowboat, waving at the travelers to follow. They take their seats on the damp wooden bench, facing him. Halfway to the isle, the ferryman lets go of the oars for a moment to throw purse, penny, and key into the lake. The water, once muddy and cloudy, has cleared as they draw away from the shore. And studding the silt of the depths can be seen a hundred offerings, each tossed in their own time into the consecrated waters. Jewels; valuables; purses large and small of decaying, flaking leather spewing their gold coins in miniature avalanches; watches, countless watches, as if guests of Le Grand B., upon nearing the red facade, deduced that time had no such measure here. Back on the bank, the horses drift off, the memory of their happenstance masters soon forgotten, breaking into a light trot toward the woods. The rowboat reaches the isle. No sooner have his passengers disembarked than the ferryman pushes off again to put away the boat. Without awaiting his return, the messenger leads the youth to the foot of the edifice. Everything seems abandoned. The rotting perron crumbles under their footsteps. The worm-eaten balustrade half vanishes beneath untrimmed ivy; daylight perforates the veranda awning in a dozen places. They have reached the door, and the messenger gives three quick raps with the knocker. They wait. From all four corners of the sky, so luminous when they first set foot on the isle, come scurrying clouds. The lake shudders in the wind that rushes whirling into the clearing's basin. Grass buckles, the ivy on the veranda quivers. So many are the gathered clouds, dark and dense, that it seems night has retraced its steps to this very spot. A single drop of rain flattens slowly in the center of a leaf, then another, and then with a sound like a ripped tarp, the entire sky turns to downpour. The horses wandering on the slope, abruptly pelted by rain, haloed in vapor by the storm, hurl themselves forestward with a final whinny. The manor shakes, the wind howls. Icy gusts smack the veranda steps as if nature herself is bent on ousting the travelers. The messenger knocks again, to no greater avail. Furious then, stunned and benumbed by torrents that lash ever harder, the two stamp their feet and beat their fists on the door. Suddenly, it gives way. They step inside. The entrance hall is deserted: no one has come to greet them. They advance into gloom barely eased by the feeble glow of an oil lamp on a chest atop a monumental staircase across from the door. Now that it has shut again, they can hear nothing of the tempest outside but a distant murmur, and the sound of water dripping from their drenched garb. Such silence in a place they know to be inhabited—the strangeness of it catches at their throats. Around them, the walls are covered in frescoes whose enigmatic charm is only heightened by what little light the lamp on the landing offers. Women with inscrutable smiles lift torches above mysteries over which the men bend. A canny play of shadows from the flight of stairs hinders the visitors from making out what dwells in the halo of painted light. As they climb the steps, other scenes tease webs of allusion that lead to similarly imperfect revelations. Upon reaching the landing, man and youth turn to take in the entrance hall in its entirety, but swaths of darkness mar the whole in too many places, and the frescoes' meaning remains elusive. The youth seizes the lamp from the chest and brandishes it, shattering the arrangement of light and shadow. At that very moment, a chorus of howls breaks out behind him. In terror, he drops the lamp. It shatters and is snuffed. The darkness is sudden and utter, and from it rises a chaos of cries, laughter, and blows, a clamor as of an asylum struck by a bolt of lightning. The youth takes a step back and trips, falling into the nothingness. At the last moment, the messenger's hand catches him.

"What is that? What did I do?"

"I don't know. But I think I glimpsed a door over there. Let's have a look!"

Groping blindly, knocking into the chest as they pass, they cross the landing and feel their way along the wall for a door. The boy's whole body is shaking; that was where the cries came from, the other side of this very partition, and beneath his fingertips, he feels it judder from the hammering of the possessed.

"I found it! Over here!"

He catches up to the messenger. The door opens, and the din abruptly stops. They step inside. Men, women—from all evidence the same who, just a moment earlier, had been engaging in such rabid bedlam—turn on them an indifferent eye. Then, after briefly considering them in silence, they calmly resume what seems to have been their sole activity before the fleeting fit of madness overcame them. Theirs is a strange deambulation, like a dance without steps, figures, or music. Threesomes, vague affiliations—remote, impassive, mute—form and dissolve with each encounter. The room is vast and devoid of all furniture; thirty or forty men and women go about at their leisure, never touching. Through sundry egressions the recent arrivals do not at first notice owing to the gloom of their surroundings—a single torch in the hands of a masked boarder, never for a moment still, is the sole source of illumination—the staff involved in the ritual constantly rotates. Of the four walls, it seems only one, the one leading to the landing, has but a single door. The other three walls, the floor and ceiling are riddled with openings—not just doorways, but breaches forced through brick and plaster as attested to here and there by rubble negligently swept along the baseboards. There are comings, goings, evasions followed by reappearances a moment later, through crevices where strips of wallpaper still flutter. Legs thrash from a ceiling full of holes, a bosom thrusts from between strips of floorboard. The man, or woman, rights themself, dusts off their clothes, and rejoins the mournful roundelay. Muffled blows, scratching, a panoply of discreet demolition noises from a corner warns that a new passage is underway. And throughout it all, lighted here and there by the masked woman, the roundelay goes on. Men and women gaze briefly, questioningly at each other, for the roundelay must never slow. No sooner do they enter than the messenger and youth take their part unthinkingly in this inextricable interlacing of pacings and gazes, which their irruption fails in the slightest to perturb; the chain has simply been extended by two more links like any other, subject to the same sibylline rules. The youth, stunned silent, as if unhoused from himself and hurled gasping into this hidden order that seems but chaos to him, opens his eyes wide as the women pass. Quietude of mind is but a struggle forgotten by the wayside, an infinitely dull ache . . . At times, in the slow whirlwind of faces where they are as but two leaves borne on a single breeze, he and the messenger cross paths. Each time, these meetings occur in conjunction with a masked officiant, and gradually an entire heavens, in which each person stands for a star, forms itself around her. Cycle by cycle, this pantomimed cosmos coincides most closely with the one the boy bears within himself, buried, disowned, disfigured a hundred times over, and disclosing itself today in its exact configuration. His temples pearl with sweat as these fatal orbits interlock ever more precisely. His lips part, babbling ancient childish conjurations, but implacably the bodies align, the forever eclipse comes to a close. Frightful, inside his head, at the center of the glacial sky, glitters the constellation of the Graybeard. Four manservants, each taking the felled boy by a limb, carry him off to one side. In falling, he has gashed his forehead on one of the cinderblocks littering the floor. One of the men stanches the boy's wound absently with a handkerchief before abandoning him, unmoving, on a heap of dresses in a dim adjoining room. The door closes; the roundelay, interrupted for a moment, resumes. Several hours go by before a slender shadow leans over the youth and cools his brow with a bit of water from a ewer.

"You, boy! Tell me you're not dead, at least?"

He opens his eyes, he asks for more water. She gives him some, he drinks greedily.

"You're hurt!"

"I don't feel any pain. Who are you? Do you live here? I can't make you out . . ."

She laughs. "I'm ugly. Another sip?"

"I'd like that very much, thank you. Say . . . the man I came with—"

"The man with the haversack? He left the dance as well. But don't worry, you'll find him. Everyone always finds what they're looking for here. You've got all the time in the world. Is there anything you desire?"

"What would that be?"

"That's up to you. But ask, and I shall obey; that's what I'm here for. If you deem me too ugly, I'll fetch you another woman. There are many women here, all of them different: no two are beautiful, nor ugly, in the same way. Or do you desire a man? No? We have old women too, and children, and animals. Everything is possible; there is nothing in the world that cannot be an object of desire, and all desire is legitimate. The only thing I cannot give you is a bed."

"What? No bed? But—"

"That's the rule: no beds. Whatever we do, we do without beds. This pile of old rags they laid you out on will have to be scattered, or else beware the Madam! No beds, no sheets, no comfort or languor, no lies. Everyone has those somewhere else already; they come here seeking something else. Of course, there are daybeds in the basement, cloakrooms, washrooms. But up here, not a single item of furniture, nothing but bodies. Objects are kept to a minimum, like this ewer, a few lamps, a handful of other things essential to our task—an ideal space, where none would think to live . . . If my ugliness is to your liking, your wish is my command. But do not be afraid to reject me: I have no pride. Feelings? Mere furniture. I dwell only in my body. What is it you wish? Your desires will be neither pure nor unclean to me. You are free to want what you want."

"Thank you, but I'm not feeling that well yet. Perhaps later."

"Do not thank me. What I say to you I would say to anyone. Are you sure there's nothing you want? Think it over. Like all women, I have breasts, and below . . ."

"No . . . later, maybe. For now, leave me alone."

"I hear and I obey."

She rises in the dark and without another word leaves the room, taking the ewer with her. The youth shuts his eyes. His head still spins slightly, but his wound no longer torments him, as if he'd gashed his forehead only in dream. At long last, he stands up and feels oddly fit and well, his head seemingly relieved from a glut of thought. To his left he hears, through the wall, sounds of the ongoing roundelay. To the right, at the rear of the room, he spots a door. He opens it and freezes on the doorsill. In each corner of this bare room, a taper has been set on the floor. A woman and a man occupy the middle. The man, an aged man with patrician features, writhes at the woman's feet. From her ankle boots done up round her black silk stockings, her lace bodice and her hair piled high, to her plump white flesh, bulging a bit in garters with their hooks and eyes, this woman seems the incarnation of the most hackneyed harlotry, and yet her face, free of all paint, wears a look of superiority, even sanctity. The man, his arms outstretched but never touching her, pleads with her in whispers. He is quite elderly, with the delicate and perfumed elderliness of the rich. Through the sheerness of his skin can be seen the fine blue veins coursing in his temples. His hands—pale, too, as if carved from marble—from which signet and wedding rings gleam, feebly busy themselves about the woman's knees. Supine, he mutters to himself some insatiable prayer. Can she even hear it? Is she even aware that a man, soon to return unto dust, drags himself through the dust at her feet? She seems far away, as much a stranger to this place as her face is to the lingerie cinching her body. The man begins to pant. Faint blue tinges his cheekbones, and his gaze grows dark at times. The youth realizes then, from the doorsill where he stands, that this is an execution; an aged heart is about to give out. The man vaguely intuits it too and accepts it. For just a little while longer, he mimes a lover's supplication, then he asphyxiates. His eyes roll backward in his head, his hand drops to the floor, from his lips comes a final hiccup; he dies. With her fingertips, the woman rectifies some imagined disarray of her coiffure, smooths a wrinkle from her stockinged thigh, and leaves the room. The boy steps aside to let her pass. A moment later, four men—doubtless the same who had borne him earlier—enter and hoist up the old man's body. They make ready to exit the opposite door. Instinctively, the boy races ahead and opens it for them. They pass before him, and he falls in step behind. In the succession of identical rooms they proceed through, the cortege stirs not the slightest emotion. Everywhere, uncanny scenes unfold in the lamplight, always tinged with sensuality, even when they seem but polite conversations between the gloved and buttoned-up; but at times, grim fornications bar the way forward. The cortege comes to a halt and waits uncomplainingly till faun has serviced nymph or any object of his fancy. Elsewhere, there is violence, murders feigned or fulfilled, whisperings more terrifying than screams, feasts of innards, gutted nudities strewn across the path. At last, the cortege reaches an empty room, vaster than all those that have come before, taken up almost completely by a pool. Torches toss glimmers on the dark water where several bodies already float. Currents from multiple outlets along the edges converge toward a central well level with the water's surface, slowly urging the corpses toward it. One shove from the steel-tipped gaff lying on the cement lip must suffice to send them over the edge into eternal oblivion. The old man's body traces the parabola of a misshapen puppet through the air; then the waters swallow him. With the four porters gone, the boy is now alone, gazing at the pool. Slowly, the body rises. Six feet from the lip, its head has already broken the surface. Now it floats limply recumbent, arms wide, head thrown back and haloed in white hair. No sooner has it resurfaced than the currents begin sweeping it toward the pit. But the boy loses patience. He arms himself with the gaff to hasten the vanishing. The flesh slides away from the steel tip at first. Finally the body, snared at the armpit, surrenders to his thrusting and lets itself be driven wellward. One by one, it passes the other derelict hulks adrift on the current. At the well's edge, it must be worked around a woman's body blocking the way. But the codger clings stubbornly to this final companion. In the icy water, their limbs knot for a moment. The youth lashes at the flesh with the gaff. He pushes, pulls, pummels, and the cadavers regretfully relinquish each other. The old man's head bashes against the rim of the well. The youth slides the gaff beneath the nape of his neck and lifts the head long enough for it to hurdle the obstacle. The body follows, catching again at the elbow, and finally topples into the darkness. The youth drops to his knees on the pool's cement lip. The sound of footsteps from near the entrance makes him look up. A figure appears in the doorway. The boy quickly gets to his feet. The messenger looks displeased.

"Well, what have you been up to?"

The boy is unsure how to respond. He shrugs and walks slowly over to his companion.

"I've been looking all over for you!"

"I fell. I hurt myself. Look, see? Then a woman spoke to me, and—"

"We came with a specific goal in mind. Do not forget that. No one here can teach you a thing." With a sweep of his hand, the messenger indicates the dead drifting slowly in the pool.

"You mean you haven't found . . . ?"

"Not yet. This house is enormous. You're going to help me. Since they haven't yet made themselves known, perhaps the one I seek lives in a secluded room? We must check everything, see everything, hear everything, ask everyone—guests and boarders alike, but also handymen and madams . . . We'll split up. Each person you meet you will ask, 'The messenger is here. To whom must he address himself?' Do you understand? Waste no time with the long-winded, the curious, the well-meaning. They know nothing."

They leave the room.

"You go that way."

The youth slips through the crack in the wall the messenger points to. He emerges on the other side powdered with plaster and undertakes to interrogate all those he meets.

"The messenger is here. To whom must he address himself? The messenger is here . . ."

They laugh, they snarl, they question him back, they yawn, they consign him to hell. Elsewhere, unconcerned with his request but delighted by his youth, men and women suggest a thousand and one carnal amusements. He pursues his quest. He opens doors, steps over bodies; faces and gazes come one after another—empty, maniacal, mocking.

"The messenger is here. To whom must he address himself?"

"We don't know, we don't care, think no more of it, come with us!"

Some hide their faces in their hands and weep. Some leap to their feet to beat and berate him; some tap their foreheads with a finger but give no reply. Others still—many, in fact—wish to know the whys and wherefores, discussing and commenting and scratching their chin at length.

"A messenger? The messenger? Ah yes, perhaps . . . A tall blond man, no? No, you say? Then I'm afraid I don't know . . . Is he the Messiah, your messenger?"

Several cross themselves despite his denials. The boy pushes on. A stairway leads him to the basement. In an enormous dormitory, on iron beds, spent boarders sleep. A few, awake, apply makeup or change clothes before small mirrors on the planks of raw wood affixed to their bedside that serve as dressing tables. One of these women rises and comes to meet him.

"Sorry, kid, but the fun and games are upstairs. You've got no business here."

"I know, but I'm looking for someone. The messenger is here. To whom must he address himself?"

"The messenger? What messenger? Never heard of him. But hold on. Ho, ladies! Yes, you! Wake up!"

She shouts into the silence of the dormitory. No doubt accustomed to such orders barked out loud, the women waken. Those going about their ablutions stop and look up. At that very moment, twenty faces turn toward them, some puffy from sleep, others half-painted, all eyes or mouth like unfinished portraits.

"This kid says a messenger's arrived, but doesn't know whom to see. That ring a bell with anyone?"

One by one, the faces betray the same expression of uncaring ignorance before falling back on tick mattresses or turning back to study themselves. The boy shrugs.

"Well, it doesn't matter. Thanks all the same. I'll try farther over that way."

"Where? All the way back over there? Nothing doing."

The woman plants herself in front of him to block his way.

"See here, this is very important. I must look everywhere."

"No way no how! Now beat it, y'hear?" The woman is big and heavy. Her face grows menacing. The small razor she was shaving herself with when he first turned up hasn't left her hand.

"Let me through, please!"

"Scram! Little prick!"

The boy feints left. Thrown off balance, the woman is unable to catch him. The razor hisses past his shoulder. He dashes between the beds.

"That little prick! Someone grab a hold of him!"

Yowling like harpies, the boarders leap to their feet, clutching at his legs, tearing at his face with their nails. He wriggles free, lashes out, slaps his share of soft white flesh that abruptly purples, finally making it through the hedge of human brambles. The door in the back wall offers no resistance. He darts through, slams it behind him, slides a bolt. Instantly the furies fall silent. Through the wall, it sounds in fact like they've scattered back to their beds, the boy's fate no longer a concern. Reassured, he takes a few steps farther into the room. Before him, on a mammoth bed of state, lies a very old woman at death's door. Like a number of the other boarders, she is dressed in fine silk whose sheerness leaves nothing of her decrepitude to the imagination. Veins bulge from what little blotched flesh still hangs from her bony frame, everything slack, lined, expiring in a face where life is now but ill-applied fard. Two young boarders attend to her, girls in summer dresses. At the youth's entrance, they rise from the old woman's bedside. Into their hands, from who knows where, spring small knives, sharp and glittering.

"Who are you? What do you want?"

"The messenger is here. To whom must he address himself? Would you know?"

The two young women keep advancing on him. He steps back. "Sheathe your knives . . . please! I—"

They hiss. Just as they are about to pounce, a fading voice stops them in their tracks.

"Leave him be! I wish to hear what he has to say. What did you say, boy? Come closer . . ."

The young women step aside. The boy approaches, and at the foot of the bed, repeats his words. With great difficulty, the old woman sits up to get a better look at him. Almost at once, her head sags backward; her voice is but a winded whisper.

"The messenger? Can it be? I know, yes . . . I am the one he seeks, I have been waiting. I have been alive for such a very long time, I have spent my whole life waiting for him. Is he truly here? You saw him?"

"I am his aide."

"His aide! How wonderful!"

"The message was meant for you, then?"

"What was that? For me? Oh, no, not me, surely you jest! No, I am a mere relay. I have but a few words to pass on to the messenger, an address to give him. But hark, where is he? Go fetch him—bring him, quick! No, wait . . . what if I were to die before he reached me? No, wait—stay! Listen closely. There is a ship in the harbor. It is called *The Crossing*. You won't forget that? *The Crossing*. I was barely as old as these two girls when it entered port. Since then, it has never left. I remember, it was the summer I turned fifteen. I was beautiful already, already a whore. The weather was lovely! Never had we seen such white sails, on so blue a sea! We girls all flocked to the quay, waiting on the sailors, speculating on their handsomeness, their generosity; we were dreaming aloud, as if such a fine ship could only be crewed by demigods. And handsome they were! So handsome they could've kept their gold, we would've given them anything, agreed to everything, and asked nothing in return. Oh, that graceful crew! Eros scrubbed the decks, Narcissus manned the tiller! And they spent extravagantly, a gold coin for a single kiss, a jewel for a caress, somber and smiling, gallant to the lowliest of us! And out of them all, I was the one the captain invited to his quarters. He wasn't one of those ephebes in sailor's blue linen who had turned our heads. No, he was a man, neither handsome nor ugly. He didn't lay a hand on me—that wasn't why I'd been summoned. He had me sit down, and he spoke to me. Not for a moment did it occur to me to refuse his proposition, although it was a commitment that would last the rest of my life. I was to join Le Grand B. as a lowly working girl. One day, a man would come—the messenger.

All I had to do was tell him he was expected aboard *The Crossing*. That was the whole of my duty. Once I had done so, a fabulous sum would be paid to me in gold, and I would be free from all obligation. But until that day came, I was never, under any circumstances, to set foot outside Le Grand B. Now you know everything. Though I have since risen through the ranks of the hierarchy within Le Grand B., which I have run for some twenty years now, I have only my own talents to thank—my artfulness in hatching ploys, my cruelty. Over time, my impatience to see the messenger at last dwindled. I still awaited him, but the fortune and freedom he was to bring me faded into the background: I had to make a living, so I made my burrow here, like any animal, where fate cast me. For a long time, in my pursuit of power, I even doubted the messenger would ever come, for that would have stripped me of my ambition. But many a year now, sure of my position and with no more but the occasional schemer to quash, I have been awaiting his arrival once more. I am dying. I have had countless men and reigned over generations of women. If I can still fulfill the task I was given in the distant days of my youth, I will have no regrets."

The old woman falls silent. After a brief spell of vigor her breathing, now already labored once more, grows shallower, in painful fits and starts. Curled up at the foot of the bed, her two favorites look asleep; abruptly they rise, leaning over the woman in the last throes of life.

"She is dying. You may fetch the dauphine," one says.

Without a word, the other girl leaves the room. The old woman seems not to have heard. Her gaze clouds, and she begins softly to ramble, a gentle delirium that mingles old memories and snatches of whispered obscenities, almost tenderly recited, like nursery rhymes. From time to time, she pauses to seek the youth's hand on her eiderdown.

"Are you there? You'll tell him, won't you? *The Crossing*, that handsome ship! You'll tell him? You won't forget?"

At the very moment she passes away the door opens, and her last breath is lost to the hinge's creaking. A woman—the very one who had put the old man to death earlier—advances toward the bed.

"It is done?"

"Just now."

"Very good. The two of you may leave."

The two young women obey, swallowing their disappointment over being dismissed at the very moment of succession.

"Why, are you still here, boy? I'd forgotten about you. Come, let me get a good look at you. How old are you?"

"I don't know."

"Old enough to take and be taken. Come."

The youth hesitates. The woman is sitting on the edge of the bed. She seizes his wrist and pulls him toward her.

"Come!"

"No, I can't. I must find my master first. I'll be back later, if that's all right."

"Forget about your master! I want it now. And so do you! Why else would your eyes glitter so? You want it! Your hands are shaking, your heart pounding. What a dumb creature you are, and handsome, blushing like that! This is your first time, isn't it? How lucky you are! Oh, how I want you!"

He surrenders. They roll around on the dead woman's body, which hangs half off the bed, head dangling, eyes open.

Unnoticed by them, the door opens, curious heads poking in. Growing slowly bolder, a crowd of boarders and their johns silently pour into the room and take up places around the bed, as if at a circus. Doubtless the news of the old woman's death, first let slip by the ousted pair of girls and then spread by word of mouth all over Le Grand B., has drawn them all, and here they are, witnessing her successor's investiture. Among them, with a front-row seat, is the messenger, with a crooked grin at his aide's prowess. The lovers untangle themselves at last. The youth rolls to one side, and in so doing unbalances the cadaver, which falls to the rug. The woman stands up. A smile hovers on her lips. She seems satisfied—if not by the boy's flagrant inexperience, at least by the effect, on those assembled, of the carnal embrace that inaugurates her long-coveted station as madam and mistress in the eyes of one and all. With a wave of her hand, she dismisses the crowd, which scatters in confusion.

"Take this carcass away."

The two young women set to the corpse, one by the arms, the other by the legs, and haul it off among the rows of beds. The door shuts once more. The woman turns to the messenger.

"So who are you? What are you doing here?"

"This boy is my servant. I was waiting for him."

The woman shrugs. Without further thought, she begins unlacing her faded bodice. The youth rises, neatening himself up.

"Well?" asks the messenger.

"It was her. The dead woman."

The messenger pales.

"Don't worry, nothing's been lost! She was only here to pass on information. You must go to the port. A ship awaits you there, *The Crossing*. She told me so herself!"

At this, the messenger seems to age ten years at once. His features grow gaunt, his shoulders slump, a thousand hitherto imperceptible lines instantly betray his age and exhaustion.

"Oh, how weary I am! And here I thought I'd reached the end . . . but no. Nothing is over, nothing is ever finished! I must set out again, seek further. My faith is worn thin as the soles of my boots. It seems I've spent my life in troubled slumber, only to wake at the moment of death. Look! My hands are shaking, my knees creaking, the hair on my head has gone white. What could I have been thinking? All that business about a message and an inspiring task? Absurd. Absurd! No, I must be asleep still, in the wee morning, I am fifteen and soon my mother will come to wake me. How many such tales I read in the tomes of my childhood, wherein the hero wakes on the final page! Stories simpleminded yet profound that I never tired of reliving, that contained the world entire . . . but bah! Come now. Here I am, everything is true. I'm expected at the port? Then to the port we shall go, and farther still if need be, so long as our legs will carry us."

The messenger gets to his feet. And totters.

"Walk, you old thing!"

He pulls himself together. With that most familiar of gestures, he settles the strap of his haversack over one shoulder. The woman, rubbing an almond-scented cream into her flesh, doesn't even look up when they leave. The dormitory is deserted; in a bed near the exit lies a woman, just one. All that can be seen of her is a black mound of hair peeking from the sheets. Man and boy have passed her and are almost at the foot of the stairs when suddenly an execration explodes from behind them, there is a hissing in the air, the messenger lets out a cry of pain and stumbles. From the flesh of his back, two fingers from his haversack strap, juts a knife. The wound is deep, blood running freely and soaking his jacket's dark fabric. Behind them, in an aisle between the beds, the boarder who tried to bar the boy's path earlier now rages at having missed her shot.

"You lucked out, kid. I was aiming for you!"

She raises a fist. It gleams with a razor she's opened in case of retaliation. The boy has already grabbed a long whip lying on a nearby bed, but the messenger stops him.

"No, no, leave it. We must hurry. Forget her. Quick, pull out the knife, and let us leave this place!"

At first, the youth refuses to drop the whip, trying to pull the knife from the wound with one hand, but he soon sees it will take two. Meanwhile, the woman prowls about, seeking an opening. She's too close. The youth seizes the whip, leaps at her, and catches her off guard, opening across her cheek a mauve rictus. The woman screams and falls back, hands pressed stiffly to the stripe on her face. Quickly, then, the youth returns to the messenger, yanks the knife from the wound, and as best he can, helps the man up. He's almost fainting.

"Master! What do we do? I can finish her off and bandage you up on one of these beds . . ."

"No. We must go, we must go now! They're waiting for me at the port. Help me up these stairs!"

They take to the stairs. The risers are steep. Soon, the messenger's face is awash in sweat. One pushing the other, they climb, leaving a little blood on every step. Up top, all is deserted. The players in the muddled dramas previously unfolding have left the stage. Torches burn all alone in the quiet of rooms where, now and then, an abandoned prop rolls away from their feet: a fan, a leather-sheathed dildo, a handful of pins in a velour case. The shutters bang, wide open on the night. Leaning out the window for a moment, the boy greedily inhales a lungful of acrid air laden with the smell of the lake.

"Come! Come!"

His master calls. They press on, the same silence greeting them wherever they go—the same shivering, half-consumed candles among rubble at the foot of the wall—and nowhere does there stir a living soul.

"But where have they gone?"

The messenger attempts a shrug, only to press his lips together in pain. "What does it matter? Let us make haste."

They push open the door to the main room, vaguely expecting to find themselves among boarders and johns. But no—the original roundelay has broken off as well, and in one corner, wedged upright between two cinder-blocks, the officiant's torch lets out a last red glow. Despite the utter darkness on the landing, messenger and youth manage to avoid the chest and make their way unhindered to the grand staircase, which they descend blindly, yet with surprising sureness of step, as if these stairs, which they have climbed but once in their lives, are suddenly as familiar to them as those in the houses of their birth. The frescoes they found so intriguing that morning—it now seems to the boy that he's always known their meaning and can describe them from memory like pictures on the wall of a childhood bedroom. They have lost their aura of terror and tragedy. The workings of his soul, revealed at last, now stir nothing in him but placid curiosity, and the as-yet inchoate desire to make of them a weapon someday. Life has no doubt never been as horrid or as beautiful as paintings have made it out to be. They reach the bottom of the stairs. Straight ahead of them, at the end of the entrance hall, the front door gapes open on the starless night. They step outside. Deep in the sky, a line of daylight stripes the horizon as if peeking out from beneath a colossal door. Man and boy shiver.

"Let's look for the rowboat. Hurry!"

They leave the perron and round the house.

"Over there, I think."

They spend some time swatting through the shrubs by the shore. Day is breaking, and above them, Le Grand B., the monster with a hundred open eyes, slowly emerges from shadow. At last they locate the rowboat, but the storm has filled it to the brim, and first they must bail it out with an absurdly tiny tin cup found bobbing by the reeds. The boy slaves away with the cup as the messenger shivers, knee-deep in silt, his voice quavery with fever when he urges haste. With one hand, he gauges the water level in the hull.

"Stop! That'll do. It's enough to get us across."

Together—for the youth knows he cannot do it alone—they haul the craft out and tumble in. At the touch of the muddy, icy water that still fills half the boat, the messenger groans. The youth seizes the oars and rows for land as best he can. Already waterlogged, the boat only grows heavier after a few yards. The messenger straightens up and starts frantically bailing.

"There's a hole in the hull! Get as far as you can. Faster! Faster!!"

The boy pulls harder on the oars, but water is rushing into the boat. In the middle of the lake, they go under.

"Where are you? Help me!"

"Here! Over here! Hang on!"

Wet dogs, bloodied dogs, they paddle about for some time in the frigid water before realizing how shallow it is. They find their footing. They set off again, panting, whimpering, biting off imprecations between chattering teeth. The bank is close, but high. The youth pulls himself up first, then turns to help his companion. It is almost light out now. Sprawled in the damp grass, they try hard to catch their breath.

"The haversack . . . Take it from my back. Hand it to me."

The boy obeys. The messenger opens the drenched haversack and takes out a cylinder of varnished wood, checking to see if it is still watertight. A smile of satisfaction lights his face for a moment: the message is intact.

"We go now. Our clothes will dry as we walk."

The youth looks up. Dark clouds hang unmoving over a drear dawn. He scowls, doubt twisting his lips. The messenger studies the sky in turn.

"We must leave this place, at any rate. Here, take this knife. Cut off a branch for me to use as a cane."

The boy lops off a bough. Meanwhile, the messenger wrings out his haversack before putting the cylinder back inside.

"Are you done? Here, hand it over. The knife, too." Swiftly, he trims the bough and carves the larger end into something like a knob. "Help me back up."

On his feet now, he puts his whole weight on the makeshift cane, testing it. "All right. Let's go."

"Which way?"

The messenger points east, away from town and Le Grand B.

"That way. We're not far from the sea now, I think."

No sooner have they taken a few steps than it begins to rain, ragelessly, in slow, fat drops that take their time dispiriting a man. Nothing in the skies portends even the slightest respite. Behind them, Le Grand B. is soon lost in grayish veils. For a long time they press on beneath the low sky, white with cold in their sodden rags; the boy coughs and the messenger moans softly, unthinkingly, as if humming. They cross through fields steaming with vapor, clamber up embankments, slosh through the mud of sunken paths, falling so often they turn into automata of flesh and turf, ill-made creatures an oafish God has botched there in the field. All around them, nature seems to drip and trickle, returning by dint of some wearied abjuration to the primordial squander of earth and water. Trees gorge on rain, hedges become brume, haystacks sag. Upon sighting a road, they hasten their step to escape at least the mud, this countryside hungry as a monstrous sponge. The tap-tap-tapping of the messenger's cane on the gleaming asphalt assures them of the solidity, fidelity, of the real world, which their being mired for too long has brought them to doubt.

"Is it much farther?"

"A few miles, I'd hazard. Does my wound still bleed?"

The messenger sits down, hunched, on a rock at the edge of the road. The youth leans over him. Under the smeared serge, blood still wells bright despite the clot blinding the cyclopean wound.

"You need tending to."

"Once we get there!"

"You won't make it. You've lost too much blood! You're bleeding out, slowly. I see a roof over there. They'll bandage you up, we can rest for a bit . . . The ship has been waiting for you so long. What's another hour or two?"

"Silence! You don't understand! This wound isn't what's killing me, it's this wooden tube swinging around in my haversack. It wounds me, it burns me, I want no more of it! I can't take it anymore!"

"Then throw it away! What difference will that make? If you toss it in the brambles, will the planets stop spinning like lights in a tavern before a drunk's eyes? And if you bring it to whomever it was meant for, what then? What will happen? Will a trumpet sound from above and the gates of Eden open to us once more? Is that what you believe?"

They scream at each other as the rain redoubles its fury. The messenger has risen to his feet. Anger, consternation are plain on his mud-spattered face.

"Of course it won't, none of it! That's not what this is about! I don't believe in anything, I don't know anything! I must bear this message. Someone is waiting for it. That certainty suffices me. Anyway, get out of here! I don't need you! Disappear!"

The boy takes a long, slow look at the flat stretch of road. He snickers. "Disappear? Where to? There? Or over there?"

He cups his hands like a speaking trumpet and, feigning a vast distance between them though they are but steps apart, shouts at the top of his lungs. "Here! I'm right here! I'm in this world too!"

"Shut up! Shut up! Go away!!" Unsteady on his legs, the messenger menaces the boy with his cane. But his anger exhausts him. He staggers and must sit back down on the rock. His heart's not in it. He keeps speaking in a low voice, as though to himself. "Get out of here. Don't hang around and be underfoot. That's all I ask of you. Leave me the hell alone!"

The youth hesitates. His voice softens, so that he speaks almost tenderly despite the harshness of his words. "I understand. I'll go. Die alone, you mangy old cur! Die, so we won't have to hear about it ever again! We'll toss you in the potter's field, you and your precious message! All your partners in crime, they're all dead already, the alderman's rival and the old lady from Le Grand B. The captain of *The Crossing* must be pretty old too . . . Everyone else will forget, even me; I'll forget. I'll find my place in the world, I'll become someone, and I'll forget this business ever happened; it'll peter out like an ill-fed brook on a thirsty plain."

He falls silent. For a moment, nothing can be heard but the sound of water, diminishing after a brief spell of renewed furor.

"Come on, get up! I'll help you."

The messenger looks on, dumbfounded, from beneath his shapeless hat, letting himself be taken and led away like a child. "As . . . as you wish . . ."

He steps forward and lays an arm around the boy's shoulders, the cane in his other hand dragging more on the ground than bearing weight. The roof they glimpsed earlier turns out, as they draw closer, to be but the tallest of six or seven in a tiny hamlet, hove close to either side of the road like knots in a rope. They stop between two identical facades, windows closed and shutters tight, and the boy sits his companion down on a milestone long since weathered bare of its numerals.

"Wait here. I'll go for help."

Too weary to protest, the messenger lets him go. The youth pushes open the gate to a pitiful yard. In a few steps he reaches the door. He knocks. No answer. He knocks again, shouting. "I've got a wounded man here!

He's lost a great deal of blood. He might die! He needs tending to!"

He seems to hear the shuffle of slippers and sees, down and to his right, a mournful face in one pane of a tall, shutterless window. Then . . . nothing. He waits a moment longer, but no one comes to the door. Shrugging, he turns back and crosses the road to try his luck on the other side. No matter where he knocks, the doors stay shut; no one even bothers to come out and shoo the troublesome vagabond from their doorstep. They simply wait for him to give up. He returns to the messenger.

"Let's go. We'll make it somehow."

They set off again. Somewhere, a dog barks, as if to say: *safe travels*. The road winds on; the hamlet vanishes. The rain, ever-present but finer than before, drowns the world around them. The messenger grows silent, wholly gathered up into himself, occupied by a single thought: the command he must unceasingly repeat to his legs to bear him up and carry him forward. After a final bend in the road, the sea appears, slapping the rocks. From afar, the gulls at play there seem spurts of sea spray touched by the breath of life. Below the cliff, the city and the port stretch away into the distance. They begin the long descent. The messenger would like to break into a run, so close does his goal now seem, but the road, after cutting straight along the cliffs, now slips down between two lips of stone, dispelling what little strength hope has mustered.

"I can't take any more. You were right. I'll never make it."

"Sure you can! Lean on me. Just a few more switchbacks, and the road runs straight into town—you'll see! It's no more than a quarter of an hour, maybe less."

It is a lie; they both know it. It is twice if not three times as far, and the messenger's wound has reopened. Blood runs from his back down his heels to thin in the puddles. He has closed his eyes, and his arm weighs heavy on the youth's shoulders. Ten times on the way down he stumbles on a rock, his whole body crumpling to the ground, and each time, the youth has a harder time convincing him to get back up. Another landscape comes ineluctably to overlie that of rocks and rain: a lake of dark water, with shores of dust or ash. To this lake the messenger comes each time he faints, stretching out beside it and drinking his fill of water that grows sweeter with each sip.

"Master! Master, wake up! We're almost there!"

No, leave me . . . I like it here. Why don't you come with me? How delicious this water is! You'd think you were sipping sleep itself . . . There, in the depths of the lake, my message awaits. We must dive fearlessly to the very bottom, and there, we shall know fulfillment!

Shouts, prayers, slaps—none of these do a thing. The messenger has sunk beneath consciousness. The boy turns the motionless body over on the embankment and bends to listen for a heartbeat. There it is . . . but so faint! He straightens up. The rain hasn't stopped; it lashes at the first facades of the city's fringe, fifty feet away. Nearer still, a sign points the way to the port. The boy hoists up the body in his arms and, panting and swearing, heaves it over one shoulder. His legs give out beneath the man's weight, and he goes down on one knee, but once he has distributed the weight more evenly, he bucks to his feet again. The messenger's head lurches forward; his hat falls off, and his hair hangs in filthy locks. From the haversack now against the boy's cheek comes the smell of drenched canvas. His steps ring out on the big cobblestones. Not a soul is to be seen, not even a dog crossing the street. As in the hamlet, all is silence and closed shutters, heavy doors he surmises are so well locked and bolted that he abandons the idea of begging for help. The city seems dead; not a sound, not the slightest sign of life, however reclusive, dwells in these identical abodes. Everything is here, nothing is missing from the scenery of a populous city: cafés, boutiques, carriage stands, all unaccountably deserted at this late morning hour. Now and then, the youth leans against a wall with his burden. Despite his cramping arms and shaking legs, he doesn't dare set it down on the sidewalk for even a moment to stretch his sore muscles, for fear of being unable to lift it back up again. As he advances, homes give way to warehouses and red-brick depots as a whiff of tides heralds the nearness of the quays. At a fork in the road, the youth unhesitatingly chooses the path that hews closest to the sea. Another hundred yards, and he has to stop: an iron gate ten feet high bars the width of the road. The guard booth looks empty on the far side of the gate, which against all expectations turns out to be unlocked. It opens when he pushes, the great cast-iron mass swinging on its oiled hinges with a squeak just softer than that of a birdcage. Beyond stretches a labyrinth of warehouses and excise offices, lazarettos, ramps strewn with wedges, handcarts, blocks and tackles. All is still, as if a murderous plague has emptied the docks of every last worker. A few masts sway behind the line of rooftops. Now and then, the wind brings, all the way to the gate, marine noises like no other: the rasp of rope on wood, a scream of timber thwarts, a splatter of water. The sky is still overcast. In his clothes soaked with rain and sweat, the youth reels beneath the messenger's weight. From crumbling crates, from every door left ajar surge rats that crowd in his wake, perhaps waiting only for him to fall to swarm him. When he shakes a fist at them, they blink but do not retreat. Some of the boldest follow him from a short distance. Beyond the last block of warehouses, the boy sees the quays. He hastens his step. A hundred sparks of light, a hundred butterflies dance before his eyes. He forces himself to the nearest wall, to lean against it, but his legs buckle and down he goes, the messenger with him. The rats rush forward, and the sight of lips bared over two rows of razor teeth, the terror of it, keeps him from fainting. With a howl that frightens the horde, he leaps back to his feet. The creatures flee, regrouping a bit farther off. They watch him in silence. The boy turns to the messenger. The body is cold and stiff, the head hanging over the gutter with its trickle of muddy water. The man died while the boy bore him on his shoulders; it happened some time ago, without his noticing. In falling, the corpse struck the edge of the curb. There, beneath a lock of hair, a violet wound streaks the man's forehead. A few drops of blood ooze idly out. The youth lifts the body to free the haversack. He opens it, takes out the cylinder of varnished wood, turning it over and over in his hands for a moment before putting it back in. Finally, he stands up and passes the strap over his head, settles the haversack snugly into the small of his back as he has seen the messenger do so many times. He walks away. The rats close in on the body with small sideways leaps. For a long moment they remain frozen beside it, hesitating, as the boy reaches the quay and disappears; then one of the rats makes up its mind. First it gives a sniff, then nibbles here and there at the flesh before sinking a tooth in deep just as the rest of the pack, reassured, rushes forward in turn. The boy walks slowly to the water's edge. At the end of the quay, moored away from the other ships, is one longer and taller, more ancient in style. He can make out the name on the stern in faded gilt letters: *The Crossing*. He stops at the foot of the gangplank and calls out.

"Ahoy! Ahoy! Is anyone there?"

After a moment, a man in blue sailor's ticking leans over the railing. "Climb aboard!"

The youth does so, soon joining the sailor. He is old, but beneath his wrinkles and sagging flesh, it is clear he was once very handsome.

"Yes?"

"I—I have a message . . . here." The boy indicates his haversack.

The sailor smiles and waves for him to follow. On deck and down in the hallways, they pass other men, all of whom look like the sailor, both in their age and the hints of a former physical grace. Everything on board is old, more than worn, but the pitted woodwork leaves not a speck of dust on the boy's finger, the brass gleams, the frayed ends of the slack and tattered rigging are farded with whiting. The sailor knocks at a door. He leads the boy through. From his desk at the far end of the cabin, the captain looks up.

"Yes?"

The sailor who guided him in steps aside. With an uncertain step, the boy approaches the desk.

"I have a message for you." He pulls the cylinder from the haversack and sets it on the desk. The elderly captain shakes his head.

"No, not for me. My crew and I are only here to take you farther."

"Where?"

"The far side of the ocean, to a certain port where people await you, perhaps to receive your message at last and answer it I know not how, or perhaps to take you farther still; truly, I do not know. It is not my affair."

"But I'm not the messenger! He didn't even give me this case! I took it from him when he died. Here I am, bringing it to you, that's all!"

"From now on, you are the messenger. Better get used to the idea. Come now, don't get all worked up; you're exhausted. Get some rest; there's a cabin at your disposal. Here, take the case back. Sailor, show the messenger to his quarters and notify the crew. We weigh anchor."

The youth follows the sailor out the door. Together, they head into the depths of the ship. All around them, gray water slaps at the hull.

Paris-Les Lecques, March–July 1973
Lozère, May–July 1989

Edward Gauvin translates from French with a personal focus on post-Surrealist literatures of the fantastic and graphic novels, of which he has translated more than 450 to date. His writing and translations have appeared in *McSweeney's*, *The Paris Review*, *The New York Times*, *Harper's*, *LitHub*, *The Kenyon Review*, and *The Saturday Evening Post*. He has received fellowships and residencies from the Guggenheim and Lannan foundations, the NEA, PEN America, the Fulbright program, and the French and Belgian governments. His debut story collection, *The Ear in All the Night*, is due out in December from 7.13 Books.

THE SCHOOL OF THE STRANGE

1. *Spells*, Michel de Ghelderode

2. *Whiskey Tales*, Jean Ray

3. *Cruise of Shadows: Haunted Stories of Land and Sea*, Jean Ray

4. *Waystations of the Deep Night*, Marcel Brion

5. *The Great Nocturnal: Tales of Dread*, Jean Ray

6. *Circles of Dread*, Jean Ray

7. *Malpertuis*, Jean Ray

8. *The Impersonal Adventure*, Marcel Béalu

9. *The City of Unspeakable Fear*, Jean Ray

10. *The Messengers*, Georges Olivier-Châteaureynaud